Promises in the dark.

"Darcy, it's been too long," he murmured against her lips before he claimed them again.

"Why do I always feel shell-shocked when you kiss me?" she whispered, not expecting or needing an answer.

He buried his face in the graceful curve of her neck. His breathing was the only sound in the darkened room, and he held her tight for several moments.

"That was to make up for bungling our wedding kiss. Now that I finally got it right, maybe I can live with myself," he explained with a slow smile. "I won't let it happen again. Unless you want it to."

"Under the circumstances," she said, "that wouldn't be a good idea."

Darcy caught a glimpse of her kiss-swollen lips in the mirror and felt the unwanted sting of tears. This was all wrong. The vows they'd spoken mocked her, that promise to love, honor and cherish. Forever. Or until the deadline was up.

Dear Reader:

Happy October! The temperature is crisp, the leaves on the trees are putting on their annual color show and the daylight hours are getting shorter. What better time to cuddle up with a good book? What better time for Silhouette Romance?

And in October, we've got an extraspecial lineup. Continuing our DIAMOND JUBILEE celebration is Stella Bagwell—with *Gentle as a Lamb*. The wolf is at shepherdess Colleen McNair's door until she meets up with Jonas Dobbs—but is he friend or the ultimate foe? Only by trusting her heart can she tell for sure.... Don't miss this wonderful tale of love.

The DIAMOND JUBILEE—Silhouette Romance's tenth anniversary celebration—is our way of saying thanks to you, our readers. To symbolize the timelessness of love, as well as the modern gift of the tenth anniversary, we're presenting readers with a DIAMOND JUBILEE Silhouette Romance each month, penned by one of your favorite Silhouette Romance authors. In the coming months, writers such as Lucy Gordon and Phyllis Halldorson are writing DIAMOND JUBILEE titles especially for you.

And that's not all! There are six books a month from Silhouette Romance—stories by wonderful writers who time and time again bring home the magic of love. During our anniversary year, each book is special and written with romance in mind. October brings you *Joey's Father* by Elizabeth August—a heartwarming story with a few surprises in store for the lovely heroine and rugged hero—as well as *Make-believe Marriage*—Carole Buck's debut story in the Silhouette Romance line. *Cimarron Rebel* by Pepper Adams, the third book in the exciting CIMARRON STORIES trilogy, is also coming your way this month! And in the future, work by such loved writers as Diana Palmer, Annette Broadrick and Brittany Young is sure to put a smile on your lips.

During our tenth anniversary, the spirit of celebration is with us year-round. And that's all due to you, our readers. With the support you've given to us, you can look forward to many more years of heartwarming, poignant love stories.

I hope you'll enjoy this book and all of the stories to come. Come home to romance—Silhouette Romance—for always!

Sincerely,

Tara Hughes Gavin
Senior Editor

PEPPER ADAMS

Cimarron Rebel

CIMARRON STORIES

Silhouette Romance

Published by Silhouette Books New York

America's Publisher of Contemporary Romance

SILHOUETTE BOOKS
300 E. 42nd St., New York, N.Y. 10017

ISBN: 0-373-08753-5

First Silhouette Books printing October 1990

Printed in the U.S.A.

Books by Pepper Adams

Silhouette Romance

Heavenly Bodies #486
In Hot Pursuit #504
Taking Savanah #600
*Cimarron Knight #724
*Cimarron Glory #740
*Cimarron Rebel #753

*Cimarron Stories

PEPPER ADAMS

lives in Oklahoma with her husband and children. Her interest in romance writing began with obsessive reading and was followed by writing courses, where she learned the craft. She longs for the discipline of the "rigid schedule" all the how-to books exhort writers to maintain, but does not seriously believe she will achieve one in this lifetime. She finds she works best if she remembers to take her writing, and not herself, seriously.

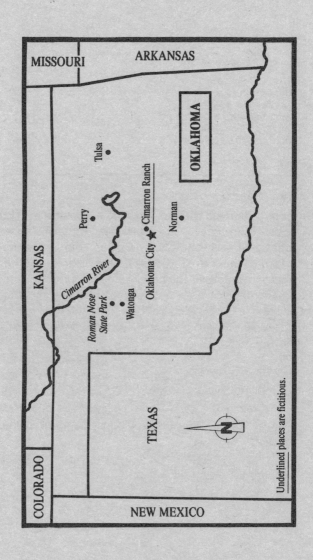

MISSOURI ARKANSAS

OKLAHOMA

Tulsa

Cimarron Ranch

Perry

Norman

KANSAS

Cimarron River

Oklahoma City

Roman Nose
State Park

Watonga

TEXAS

N

COLORADO

NEW MEXICO

Underlined places are fictitious.

Chapter One

"Will I marry you?" Darcy Durant repeated the question with an indignant sputter and glared across the table at the cocky cowboy who'd dared to ask it. Just in case tone alone did not convey the full extent of her amusement, she added, "When pigs fly!"

"Keep your voice down, Darce. People are starting to stare at us." Grinning his professional bad-boy grin, Riley Sawyer glanced around the small smoky club. Aptly called the Dust Bowl Lounge, it was crowded with cowboys, rednecks and other lovers of country music.

He figured Darcy would have reservations about his unheralded proposal, but he hadn't expected such a flat-out rejection. Not after he'd explained how much he'd changed. A recovered alcoholic, he no longer sought ease from a bottle. It had been nearly a year since he'd last seen Darcy, and he'd learned a lot about himself.

There was more to rehabilitation than beating dependency and he'd gone the whole nine yards. He'd finally learned to face his problems and deal with them; no more desperate detours through Margaritaville. He was a new man. In fact, he was so upstanding he hardly recognized himself anymore.

Riley's shushing increased Darcy's self-consciousness. She saw Mac eyeing them from behind the bar. In the two weeks she'd been moonlighting from her job at the bank by singing at the Dust Bowl, the burly owner/bartender/bouncer had shown her a fatherly protectiveness. The man tensed, bar rag in hand, ready and willing to toss her would-be suitor, or assailant, as Mac perceived him, out on his duff. She just had to say the word.

But she couldn't. She was twenty-six years old; she could take care of this herself. Her smile was long-suffering, her wave halfhearted, but she hoped the gestures would tell Mac that all was well. No problem here. Nothing she couldn't handle anyway. Just an old broken heart come back to haunt her.

Reluctantly she returned her attention to the only man she'd ever loved. Had he changed as much as he claimed? Despite the fact that his drink of choice was now lemon-lime soda on the rocks, Riley looked remarkably the same.

He still had the same brown hair crisped with gold, the same hopeful brown eyes, the same charmer's smile. Riley had done some hard living in his thirty-three years, but his boyishly handsome face bore none of the darkness of his excesses.

He was a quarter-horse trainer and he wore the official cowboy uniform with easy grace—tight blue jeans, fancy boots, cattleman's hat. Only the shirt varied and tonight it was black with embroidery on the western yoke.

Changed? If anything, after giving up hope of seeing him again, Darcy was more vulnerable to him. Whatever the reason, she felt her hard-held anger dissolve, her good intentions weaken. Riley Sawyer might be a new man, but he still wielded that old power over her senses. A power she must not submit to.

"Still going for shock value, I see." She attempted to edge her words with a harshness she didn't really feel.

"You know me, Darce. I like to get straight to the point."

"You have a lot of nerve, waltzing in here after all this time like nothing ever happened. How dare you spring something like this on me?"

Riley plunked his hat down on the tiny table and raked a hand through his hair as though the action might jump start his brain. He wished he could go out into the August night, take a deep breath of hot Oklahoma air and come back in. Maybe if he started over, he could do this better.

"It wasn't easy," he admitted.

Something in his tone tugged at her heart and she looked down. She should have figured out a way to avoid this confrontation. This pain.

"You ran away," she accused.

"Yes."

"If I remember correctly, we'd just made love and—"

"Don't, Darcy. Please."

Hurt molded Riley's features with sincerity. Now *that* was different. "Oh, but I must," she continued in a vehement whisper that helped her regain a sense of purpose. "To be sure I remember correctly. I was cooking breakfast and you were nuzzling my neck. Am I on track here?"

Riley didn't need to be reminded. He recalled that terrible morning clearly. He'd replayed it in his mind a thousand times during the past year. At the time it had seemed like the end of everything. In truth, it had been the beginning of his salvation.

Darcy ignored the regret in his eyes. She had self-preservation to think of. "We'd given ourselves to each other completely the night before. And fool that I was, I believed you when you said you'd never experienced anything like it."

"I meant it. Every word of it," Riley assured her. God, it was good to see her again. Her long black hair curled wildly around her shoulders, as untamed as her spirit. She wore a beaded denim vest over tight black pants stuffed into outrageous lavender snakeskin boots. No one could carry off lavender boots quite like his Darcy.

He wanted to take her into his arms and tell her that during the past year his love for her had been the one constant thing in his life. The thing that had made him fight his way back. But he couldn't. His desire for her was still so strong it would surely frighten her. It frightened him.

During his stay in the private clinic in Dallas he'd thought of Darcy every day and prayed that she understood what he was doing. During those long weeks a lot of things had come into focus—all the mistakes he'd made, all the opportunities he'd missed.

Every day he was reminded that he'd once possessed, however briefly, the precious gift of her love. Turning his back on that love had been the hardest thing he'd ever done. Now after months of physical healing and emotional searching, he felt worthy of what she'd offered. He meant to reclaim it, to rebuild their relationship and make it stronger than before. But first he'd have to prove to Darcy that she could trust him enough to risk her heart again. This time he wouldn't break it.

But that kind of trust took time, and Riley was short on time right now. He reached across the table to take her hand. "It'll be different now."

Steeling herself against the surge of emotions his touch provoked, Darcy withdrew her hand and went on as if he hadn't spoken. "That morning I was giddy with happiness. Like my mother, I thought my love could change you. I should have known better. It never changed my father."

"But I have changed," he said emphatically. "That's why I'm here."

"You're late, Riley. Almost a year too late."

"Don't tell me that."

Reinforcing her resolve, Darcy shook her head. If only she could shake off the memories as easily. "I told you I loved you, that I wanted to marry you. Do you recall your response to that announcement?"

He drew a ragged breath. He would never forget. Torn inside out by the memory of how he had hurt her, he searched Darcy's eyes, an unwilling accomplice to her pain. He said nothing. Words could never undo the damage he'd done that morning.

Darcy filled the uneasy silence. "You left so fast you practically left skid marks on the linoleum."

"My behavior was inexcusable. Of all the mistakes I've made, I regret that one most of all."

"That was the last I heard from you," she reminded.

"I left because I loved you."

"Yeah," she said dryly, "that's what I figured."

"I was a mess, Darcy. A complete washout as a human being. I'd let alcohol make my decisions for so long I couldn't think on my own anymore."

"So you ran?"

"I had to. At that moment, I was dangerously close to marrying you."

"Ah, yes, the fate worse than death."

"Only for you," Riley said quietly, his eyes moist with emotion. "I stood there in your kitchen, with sunshine all around, and I knew I wasn't good enough for you. I didn't want you to have me like that. Like a piece of damaged goods marked 'for sale as is.'"

"I was willing."

"But I wasn't. If I'd married you then, I would only have hurt you."

"Lucky for me total rejection is so painless," she said with a heavy dose of sarcasm.

"I was scared. For the first time in my life, I took a hard look at myself. I didn't like what I saw. After I left that morning I started drinking, and the next thing I knew my brother, Brody, was bailing me out of jail. The charge was drunk and disorderly, but the crime was years of denying the problem."

"Poor Riley." It was difficult to hang on to the bitterness when all she wanted was to believe. "Self-analysis can be hell."

"Can't you forgive me, Darcy?" His expression was all earnest hope and heart-wrenching candor.

"No." There, that wasn't so hard. She said it again to strengthen her position. "No, I can't. You ran away and you left me behind to clean up the mess you made of my life. I offered you everything, and you wouldn't let me help you. I can't forgive that."

Riley looked down at his hands.

"When I heard you went back to Ruidoso with Brody, I thought I would die. I knew how important the All-American Futurity was to both of you, to Cimarron. But you had no right to leave without a word."

"No, I didn't. But I couldn't face you in the shape I was in. I was too ashamed." The confession cost him, but he'd made up his mind before coming here tonight. Pride be damned.

Darcy saw the naked longing on his face and was filled with the old need to gather him into her arms, to comfort him as she had so many times before. She ached to hold him close and whisper sweet assurances. It was Riley's nature to inspire protectiveness in a woman and it was hers to give it.

But tempting as it was, the urge had to be resisted. She'd thought herself over the heartache, but she'd been wrong. Seeing Riley again, so perfect and repentant, brought it all back as fresh as the moment. She couldn't afford to let the man who'd caused her pain unrivaled in even the saddest country-western song lyrics back into her life. She'd loved him and he'd left her. End of song.

Ironically at that moment, someone plugged quarters into the jukebox. Riley leaned close and spoke over the recorded anguish. "I was wrong to go, but at the time I didn't know what else to do," he admitted. "Maybe it was the clear mountain air of New Mexico, but I finally sorted things out. I tried to call you once I got my act together, but by then you'd left for Nashville."

"Two can play the game, Riley."

He sighed. "I felt lost. Deserted."

He interrupted her angry protest. "I didn't say I had a right to feel that way, only that I did. I knew why you left and I understood."

"How magnanimous of you."

"But understanding didn't lessen the hurt."

"Good," she said flippantly. "I'd hate to think the suffering was all one-sided."

"I'm willing to spend the rest of my life making things up to you."

"Even with modern medical advances, no one lives that long, cowboy."

Riley flinched at this new hardness. Had he put it in her? Darcy had always been sassy and outspoken, but she'd never been cruel. "It used to be so good between us, Darcy. You loved me once."

"Loved. Past tense. I knew when you walked out that you'd call once you sobered up. That was your style. But I also knew I couldn't sit around and wait anymore."

"In a way, Darcy, your leaving was the best thing that happened to me."

"I'm glad to know I was able to help out."

"When you left Oklahoma, I realized just what I'd thrown away. It was a turning point for me. At the clinic, the counselor made us tell the precise moment when we knew we'd hit bottom. For me, letting you go was that moment. Then, when the horse Brody and I trained won the Futurity, I started to think it might not be too late for me to salvage my life."

"So you bought a racehorse."

Riley grinned. "Rebel's Redemption. I got him in a claiming race at Ruidoso. It was a gamble, but with Brody's help it's paying off. The horse has made me a pile of money this year. I've settled my debt to Brody. I've squared things with my folks. Now I want to make things up to you."

"Maybe I don't want to be on your list of Things to Do Today." Darcy knew all about Riley's comeback. Her best friend, Noelle, had married Brody Sawyer shortly after Riley checked into the rehab program.

Darcy had driven in from Nashville for the wedding, but Riley was not in attendance. According to Noelle, he was having a hard time in detox and was in no condition to travel. He didn't want his family and friends to see him until he recovered from the effects of withdrawal.

By the time that happened, Darcy was back in Nashville, pursuing a singing career. After that, she never asked about Riley in her letters and calls to Noelle, and her friend respected her decision enough not to mention him.

She hadn't planned to return to Oklahoma; she'd never wanted this meeting. With a soft sigh, she looked at the man across the table and wondered what in the world the Fates had been thinking of.

"Even though you were far away," Riley said, "you helped me through some rough times. Brody told me you wanted to be left alone, so I didn't try to contact you. But now that you're home and not involved with anyone else, I'd kind of hoped it was a sign we might still have a chance."

"No. It's a sign that lightning really can strike twice in the same place. I'm back in Oklahoma for one reason, Riley. My family needs me. Mom can't live alone since Aunt Bertie got married and moved away, and I don't want my brother dropping out of medical school."

Riley tried another tack. "I haven't had a drink in almost a year now. I'll never take another. If you have any leftover feelings for me at all, we could try again."

She felt her eyes mist over. That was a bad omen. Riley sounded so contrite, so sincere, it was hard to shut him out of her heart. But only a fool would let herself be hurt by the same man twice. "If a chance is what you want, you picked a strange way of asking. A marriage proposal presumes way too much."

"I know you need time to—"

"There'll never be enough time, Riley. A broken heart doesn't heal up like a skinned knee."

Knowing she had plenty of reason not to trust him, he pressed on, panicked by his fear of losing her for good. "I need your help, Darcy. Did Noelle tell you my ex-wife died a few months ago?"

She nodded. Riley and Candi had been married for five years, but were divorced for the past three and he had kept in touch with his stepchildren. Riley had introduced Darcy to the children and brought them along on a couple of outings but their reception of her had been cool. However, when Darcy heard about the woman's tragic death in a car crash, she'd sent written condolences to the children. "It was a terrible loss for Tyler and Jamaica."

"I'm worried about them. They've been through so much in their short lives. Did Noelle also mention that I'm trying to get custody?"

"Yes, but what's that got to do with asking me to marry you?"

"They're the reason I'm asking *now*. Their Aunt Marsha has four kids of her own and it's been a hardship for her to take in Tyler and Jamaica. She's willing to give me guardianship, but only if I remarry."

Slowly understanding dawned, and Darcy cursed herself for beginning to believe the smooth talk, for thinking things had changed. He was still the same old manipulating Riley, still up to tricks. Why did he have to spoil it? She folded her arms across her chest and leaned back. "Now I get the picture."

"Wait, Darcy, don't jump to conclusions. Marsha knows I'm off the sauce but she feels I can't give them a real home unless I'm married.

"And that's where good old Darcy Durant comes in, huh? You want me to be the other part of the equation."

"Who better?" he asked with the grin she'd seen so often in her dreams.

"Thanks, but no thanks, Riley."

"Marsha's overwhelmed by the kids. You know how difficult they can be. If I don't take them, she's talking of placing them in foster care."

Darcy's flaring anger was snuffed by Riley's quiet announcement, but she knew better than to relent. If she didn't keep her heart hard and safe, Riley would just break it again.

She sat up straighter and took on a dismissive air. This ill-fated meeting was about to be adjourned. "I wish you luck in your matrimonial quest, but I don't think you have a very strong case for marriage. A shaky one won't provide the stability those kids need."

"I won't let them go to a foster home," he said firmly.

"The system's not as bad as it was when you and Brody were in it," she told him, knowing he had good reason to keep his stepchildren out of foster care. "Isn't it?"

"I know you had it rough after your mother died and your father abandoned you, but you and Brody ended up with Dub and Ruby Roberts. They turned out to be terrific parents."

Darcy knew the story; Riley had told her often enough. The Robertses had provided the only real home the boys had ever known, as well as the only love. The old horseman and his wife taught Riley and Brody about quarter horses and helped them start their own training stables when they were ready. Riley loved and respected his foster parents and he never failed to acknowledge how much he owed them.

"There's no guarantee that Tyler and Jamaica will be as lucky," he pointed out.

"There are no guarantees in life," she reminded him. "Why don't Dub and Ruby take the kids?"

"They offered, but Marsha thinks they're too old to cope with a thirteen-year-old girl and a nine-year-old boy. Besides, they're my responsibility now. Their biological father divorced Candi and skipped town right after Tyler was born, and no one has seen or heard from him since. I may not be much, but I'm the only father they've ever known. I'm worried what will become of them. I have to do something.''

His words touched Darcy. Then she thought, No, don't let him do it. Don't listen to him. He has a problem, but it has nothing to do with you. "I hope you can convince Marsha to change her mind. Or failing that,'' she added with a tight smile, "I hope you find another candidate.''

He reached across the table and stroked her cheek. "Is that what you want me to do, Darcy? Find someone else?''

She fought the longing in his soft caress, but felt herself turn into it like a tender plant deprived of rain. She'd been parched and desolate in the months without Riley, and his touch restored some of the joy he'd taken with him. She had so few needs: air to breathe, food to eat, water to drink, Riley to love.

Impossible. "Do what you must. Just don't put the responsibility off on me.''

He cupped her face in his hands. "I'd give anything for the time it would take to convince you that I've changed. But I don't have that luxury.''

Sensing her empathy from the way she trembled, Riley pressed further, making a snap decision he hoped he wouldn't live to regret. "If you'll agree to marry me, you only have to stay long enough for me to satisfy Marsha and the courts.''

"Wouldn't that be dishonest?''

"Maybe. But I'm desperate. I can't let those kids get caught up in the system. Maybe not all foster parents abuse or neglect their charges, but it's a terrible thing for a child to know that his foster parents might be feeding and caring for him only for money. That he's just a job to them. A child needs love and permanence. Foster homes can't give that."

He took a breath and continued. "When the going gets tough, it's the kid who has to get going. I know. Tyler and Jamaica are already insecure. That kind of life would finish them. I want them to know I'm taking them because I love them and no other reason. If I have to be dishonest to the authorities to do that, so be it."

"What you want to do is admirable, Riley. But I can't be a part of it."

"I know it's asking a lot, but if you'd just give me six months as my wife it would solve a lot of problems."

Riley hoped six months would be long enough for him to prove his love for her. But would it give him time to court her when she was so dead set against it?

Darcy said nothing, so he took her hand in his and continued. "It must be hard on you. Working full-time. Singing in clubs at night. Taking care of your mother. That doesn't leave much time for yourself."

"Then you understand why I can't take on any more responsibilities."

"I can help."

"How?"

"As your husband, I'd naturally assume your financial burdens. I'll pay off Ida's medical bills and hire a live-in care giver for her. Also, as Cord's brother-in-law, I'd be happy to supplement his scholarship and help with his expenses.''

"That sounds suspiciously like bribery," she pointed out.

"Call it an incentive bonus," he said with a slow smile.

"I know training winning quarter horses is a lucrative business, but do you have any idea of the magnitude of the expenses you'd be taking on?"

"I've done pretty good this year. I could use a few more deductions."

His grin still had a way of sneaking up on Darcy, of nibbling at the fragile edges of her defenses. "I take it you heard I was a complete flop in Nashville?"

"I'd hardly describe selling two songs a flop."

"The critics did. They said that 'while Darcy Durant has a certain charm and talent, her voice is too similar to the star K. C. Maguire's for Ms. Durant to achieve national recognition.' Unquote. My agent advised me to keep writing songs and go back to my day job."

"So how's it going at the bank?" Riley knew music was Darcy's first love. Her heart never had been in customer service.

"They were good enough to take me back."

Enough small talk. "Marry me, Darcy."

"No." God help her, she wanted to say yes. She loved him so much that even when logic intervened, she waivered.

"A fresh new start," he said. "That's all we need."

They'd had those before. Each broken promise, each defection, had hurt Darcy more than the one before. The day she'd professed her love for him and he'd made tracks out of her life was the day she'd sworn never to let him hurt her again. And a promise was a promise. Even to herself.

When her mother had encouraged her to try her luck in Nashville, she'd jumped at the chance to get away from Riley for good. But all the miles and days and weeks hadn't made much difference. He'd haunted her nighttime dreams and daytime fantasies long after she should have been over him.

She hadn't come back to Oklahoma for Riley, she reminded herself. She'd come back for her family. When Aunt Bertie got married, Cord talked of giving up his scholarship to work full-time and help out at home, but Darcy wouldn't hear of it. He had a promising future as a surgeon and she meant for at least one member of the family to have his dreams. She'd managed to convince Cord that the Nashville life-style didn't suit her. That she was ready to give up on it and come home to be with their mother. So she'd returned. To her old home. Her old job. Her old losses.

Since then, her worries and financial obligations had multiplied like unseen dust balls. She'd had to work overtime at the bank and take singing jobs she didn't want. It was rough, but it was no reason to marry Riley.

"I'm not trying to buy your love," he insisted. "I respect you too much for that. We can't change the past, Darcy, but the future is ours to do with as we will."

"That's one way to look at it," she remarked, uneasy that he was beginning to make sense. "On the other hand, maybe we should learn from the past and not repeat our mistakes."

She sounded so bitter. "Do you hate me that much?"

"I don't hate you at all, Riley." But she wasn't ready to admit that despite everything she still loved him.

"Then what's wrong with friends helping friends? We need each other."

"I don't know." How could she even consider marrying him? But even as she asked the question, Darcy knew that was exactly what she was doing.

Considering.

Riley's hopes surged. He couldn't buy her, but he could buy time, couldn't he? Time to win back her love. "I won't ask you to be my wife in the biblical sense. We'd be married in name only."

"You mean like a marriage of convenience?" she asked doubtfully.

"Exactly. I'll make no emotional or physical demands on you, if that's the way you want it. And at the end of six months you'll be free to go on your way." Maybe, he hoped, at the end of six months she wouldn't want to go away.

"I don't know." If she refused, she would lose the only man she'd ever loved, for he'd made it clear that he wanted a wife. And since she could never love another man the way she loved Riley, she'd be losing a real chance for a future with him.

But if she accepted, monetary gain must not enter into her decision. She would marry Riley because she loved him and always would. "I don't know if it would work. We were always so—"

"Passionate?" he supplied with a rogue's wink. "We'll just have to be strong."

"Well..."

Riley could only hope that he could prove himself and she would never want to leave. "Who knows, we might find married life becomes us and decide to keep the knot tied permanently." His light tone belied the serious intent behind the suggestion.

"Not very likely." It hurt that he'd asked her to marry him for all the wrong reasons. But it was even more disturbing that she could accept for all the right ones.

Riley saw her waiver and took it as his cue to press for a decision. "Help me, Darcy."

Love didn't stop the worry. Life with an alcoholic father had taught her that addictions were a lifelong battle. Was this new Riley strong enough for the fight? Without giving away her thoughts, she asked, "What about Tyler and Jamaica? They've never liked me much and they might resent such an arrangement."

"They'll come around once we're married. For all their problems, they're not bad kids. They need love, stability and a little discipline. We can give them that."

"I'm not too sure of my parenting skills."

She was considering his proposal, and Riley tried not to let his elation show. "It can't be that hard. People with no training at all do it every day. Say you'll marry me, Darcy."

She struggled with uncertainty. Riley hadn't spoken much of love, but if she agreed to his crazy scheme, it might happen. In the meantime, she could make a home for him and two motherless children. She could help her mother and keep her brother in medical school where he belonged.

If she said no, Riley might fall off the wagon, and Tyler and Jamaica could end up in an orphanage. Because she couldn't afford proper medical care, her mother's arthritic condition could worsen. And Cord, instead of becoming a talented surgeon, might end up in a funny hat, asking people if they wanted fries with that burger.

All in all, saying yes was the noble thing to do. But somehow she'd always pictured the moment differently. Why couldn't it have taken place somewhere more romantic than the Dust Bowl Lounge with a rockabilly crooner supplying the musical background?

Then again, maybe it was fitting. A sham proposal for a sham marriage. Lord, what was she letting herself in for?

"I'll marry you, Riley." Darcy uttered the words with a profound sense of sealing her own fate.

Chapter Two

One week later, on a hot August Friday, wedding vows were read and repeated in a civil ceremony in the Oklahoma County Courthouse. When Riley and Darcy were pronounced husband and wife, the groom pulled the bride into his arms for the requisite kiss.

The enormity of the event, combined with Riley's nerve-rattling nearness made Darcy bob up for the kiss, bumping his nose hard with her head. He drew back with a pained grimace and watering eyes.

The kiss he planned, the one destined to make her knees weak, was replaced by a self-conscious peck as brief and unromantic as the ceremony had been. And as uninspired.

The witnesses, who were strangers recruited from nearby offices, chuckled at the couple's postnuptial jitters. Darcy begged Riley's pardon and he wiggled his nose to prove it was still attached. The judge rolled his eyes, signed the license and it was over.

Riley clutched Darcy's hand and led her out of the cool courthouse and into the suicide heat of late afternoon. Darcy allowed herself to be propelled across the parking lot, all the time wondering when she'd start feeling married and stop feeling awkward and sad. From the time she'd been old enough to plan trousseaux for her dolls, she'd fantasized about her own wedding day. What had just transpired was definitely not any girl's ideal.

"Well, we're married," Riley announced unnecessarily as he climbed behind the steering wheel of his pickup truck.

"So the man said." Her voice sounded far away, exactly where she wanted to be just now. She glanced sideways and saw him watching her with scorching intensity. Who was this man? The lost months had made him a stranger.

She had since amended her original assessment made last week in that dark cowboy club. Daylight and further discussion revealed the extent to which Riley had changed. He wasn't a fun-loving, irresponsible kid anymore. He was calm, mature. Steady and intimidating. Definitely intimidating.

He was a virile physical presence that overwhelmed and thrilled her. Better looking than she remembered. Funnier, sexier, stronger. More of all the good things he'd always been. Life really was full of surprises. Only a week ago he was gone forever and today he was . . . what?

Her husband. She groaned.

"Try not to act so thrilled, Darcy," he grumbled as he turned on the ignition. "So much enthusiasm might make people think you're happy about being married to me."

"I'm sorry. It's just that I've always thought of weddings as organ music and bouquets and pink bridesmaids' dresses. Ours had all the sentimental romance of a city councilman's swearing-in ceremony."

"And whose fault is that?" He pulled the truck into the mainstream of rush-hour traffic. "If you'd agreed to invite our families, it might have been more festive." More real. A little tossed rice would have gone a long way in the reality department.

"I didn't want Mom and Cord to witness this sham. It was hard enough without them gushing all over us."

Riley stiffened beside her and a muscle twitched in his jaw. She wondered what he was thinking. He hadn't talked much. Was he sorry already? Had he come to regret their marriage almost before the ink was dry on the license?

She wanted to turn back the clock to that second when he'd been about to kiss her. Just before she'd bopped him in the nose, she'd seen raw emotion in his eyes. She'd hoped it was desire, but now she wasn't so sure. Maybe it had been plain old fear.

"Well, Mrs. Sawyer, let's get this weekend honeymoon show on the road. Since we don't pick up Tyler and Jamaica until Monday, we'll have to think up ways to keep ourselves entertained until then." Ways to keep their hands busy.

"What did you have in mind?" she asked warily.

"Let's start with dinner at Nico's." He steered expertly around a slow moving van. He could think of a hundred entertainments, but since all of them were of a distinctly physical nature, they'd better make it a real long dinner.

"Sounds good," she agreed with more enthusiasm than she felt. She hadn't eaten since yesterday and she still wasn't hungry. Worrying about what would happen when they got to the home they were to share precluded all thoughts of food.

The owner met them at the door of the elegant restaurant. Pumping Riley's hand he said, "Congratulations, bridegroom." Turning to Darcy, Nico bowed formally and placed a kiss on her knuckles that was as continental as his dark good looks and accented voice. "I am honored to meet you, Mrs. Sawyer. Your husband is a very lucky man."

Riley gazed at his new wife with admiration. She'd passed up the traditional bride white in favor of a summer suit the color of pink champagne. The tight skirt was short enough to show off her legs and the form-fitting jacket flared at the waist with a double row of ruffles.

Riley hugged her close and beamed with what amounted to a convincing show of affection. For a moment Darcy allowed herself to get caught up in the make-believe. What would it hurt to pretend for a little while that they truly were a couple in love?

Nico led them to a darkened alcove where soft violin music wafted from hidden speakers. The table was set with crisp white linen and thin-stemmed crystal that reflected the light of delicate tapers. Red roses, arranged artfully in a short vase, added their own romance. All in all, a vast improvement over the Dust Bowl.

As soon as they were seated a waiter appeared with a bottle of champagne. "Compliments of the owner," he told them.

Riley saw Darcy's look of alarm and felt a moment of annoyance that she had so little faith in his ability to say no. "Tell Nico we appreciate it," he told the waiter smoothly. "And please bring me a bottle of mineral water."

Darcy sensed Riley's irritation and wondered if she should apologize for thinking the worst. She decided that would just draw attention to the problem and sat in uneasy silence until the waiter brought the water. "I'll have water, also," she said.

Riley frowned, and his dark eyes conveyed far more than his words. "You can have champagne, Darcy. The sight of someone else drinking won't undo all the progress I've made."

Although the words were spoken kindly, the rebuke in them was evident and Darcy felt duly chastised for her lack of faith. "Have you forgotten? I don't drink."

"See how perfect we are for each other," he said lightly to clear the air. "A teetotaler makes a great mate for a reformed alcoholic."

They made a toast and then looked over the menus. Considering all the water under their respective bridges, it was strange that they were reduced to discussing entrées like people on a hesitant first date.

"This is a little weird, isn't it?" she asked after several quiet moments.

Riley looked around the room and saw nothing amiss. "Don't you like this place?"

"Not the place. Us. We're weird."

"Really? The way heads turned when we walked in, I thought we were kind of a cute couple."

Cute wasn't exactly the word she would have used to describe her new husband. All six feet of Riley looked magnificent in a dark gray suit. His white shirt showed off a subtly striped tie, the first she'd ever seen him wear. His one cowboy concession was a pair of black diamond-toe boots. This man wasn't cute.

He was dangerous.

Riley caught her staring and she grinned self-consciously. "I feel strange sitting here with you. I know we're married and all, but I don't really know you anymore."

He took the menu from her and cradled her hands in his. "You know me better than anyone ever has or ever will, Darcy."

His holding her hands seemed too intimate for such a simple gesture and she wanted to extract them before his nearness made her forget this was all make-believe. "I don't know what to say or how to act. I've never been married before."

He smiled reassuringly. "This isn't an easy marriage to get used to. But something I learned from AA is you have to take things one day at a time."

"It's probably a good thing we didn't take time to really think about it," she rationalized.

"That's right," he agreed. "Marriage is like a cold swimming hole. It's no good to ease into it gradually. You have to hold your nose and jump in feet first." And come up breathless.

She laughed at his cockeyed analogy. "Speaking of noses, how's yours?"

"Tender, but tough. Like me."

"Oh, Riley. Are we crazy?"

"Maybe everyone who gets married is slightly psycho." When she grimaced he added, "Look, Darcy, it's okay to feel awkward, we're entitled. But it's going to work."

"Says who?" she asked, her voice an unsure whisper.

"Says me."

Darcy had visited the Sawyer ranch, Cimarron Training Stables, before. But this was no visit and she looked at her new home as though seeing it for the first time.

Riley and Brody were partners in the 160-acre facility where some of the top quarter horses in the nation were trained and housed. The ranch, situated on a rolling plain ten miles east of the city, was a small community unto itself.

Besides the barns, stables, tack rooms and training track, there was a small house where their top hand, Billy Sixkiller, and his wife lived, a number of trailer homes for the other married hands and a bunkhouse for the bachelors.

Brody and Noelle and the twins lived in a sprawling rock-and-cedar house set well back from the road. It was separated from Riley's home by a dense stand of oak and hickory.

When the truck whizzed past the graveled drive that led to the red brick traditional set among towering trees, she looked up in surprise. "Where are we going?"

"Up to the main barn."

"You're going to work? Even for someone as newly conscientious as you, that's a bit much."

"Not work. There's a little surprise waiting for us."

"What kind of surprise?"

He didn't have to answer because she soon found out for herself. A large refreshment tent was set up in front of the barn, and a party in their honor was in full and noisy swing.

Riley grinned sheepishly as he parked the truck among all the other vehicles. "What can I say?" he asked over the din of a rowdy country-western band twanging out dance music.

"I thought we weren't going to make a big deal out of this."

"Blame it on Brody and Noelle."

They walked up to the barn, and Darcy smiled as the hosts in question greeted them.

"What took you so long?" Brody wanted to know. He was taller and heavier than Riley, and his hazel eyes and dark brown hair were unlike his younger brother's. But the grins were the same and the voices pretty darn near.

"Really, Brody," Noelle teased. "Has it been so long since our honeymoon that you've forgotten how newlyweds can linger over dinner, just gazing into each other's eyes?" The blonde's petite delicacy was the perfect counterpoint to her husband's rugged masculinity.

Noelle, who was obviously pregnant, hooked arms with Darcy and Riley and led them toward the celebration. "Everyone's dying to congratulate you. Just wait until you see who's here."

Riley took one look at the crowded barn and decided the guest list must have included half the population of the county. Dub and Ruby were talking in a corner with Darcy's mother, Ida. Her brother, Cord, was dancing with the pretty daughter of a Remington Park racetrack executive. Riley's foster sister, Glory, was also dancing. Ignoring the fast tempo of the music, she and her husband, Ross Forbes, were swaying cheek to cheek.

All the hands and their families were present, as were most of the jockeys who had ever worn Cimarron's green and gold silks. Fellow trainers, breeders and owners were out in force, to say nothing of old friends.

A table in the corner, piled high with beautifully wrapped gifts, reminded Riley that he was well and truly married. All these people had come to eat wedding cake and celebrate that marriage. If he'd needed a reality check, this was it.

Ushered into the receiving line, he and Darcy were lavished with greetings and well-wishes. Caught up in the party spirit, he smiled broadly and put his arm around his bride's waist. Kissing her at the request of a camera-snapping guest, he whispered in her ear, "Try not to look so glum, Darce. We're the happy couple, remember?"

"I remember," she answered softly. She was dismayed by so much merrymaking. The deal she and Riley had concluded this afternoon at the courthouse didn't merit such celebration. But she couldn't tell her friends and family that, so she plastered a wan smile on her face as the endless line of guests bid them well.

Brody appeared and handed Riley and Darcy glasses filled with punch. Riley looked uneasily at the contents, but a nod from his brother let him know that the drink was nonalcoholic. Then Brody motioned for silence and held his glass aloft.

"A toast to the newlyweds. May they live happily ever after."

Glasses clinked and a cheer went up all around them. When things got quiet, Riley turned to Darcy. He gazed down at her with a tender look in his eyes that was sure to convince the guests that such a future was possible. It might have fooled her, too, if she hadn't known better.

"To my bride," he said in a husky tone loud enough for everyone to hear. "Thank you for giving meaning to my life."

She smiled up at him, almost lost in the moment. Maybe things would work out, after all. Could a man say that and not mean a little of it? Maybe his gratitude would eventually grow into love.

She blinked, and a lone tear trailed down her cheek. Riley kissed it away, and her heart quickened. As she touched her glass to his, she said, "I hope you won't regret it."

"Never." His declaration was as strong and sure as an Oklahoma wind.

Before long, they left the receiving line for the dance floor. It was hard on Darcy's nerves to be so near Riley, but she needed to feel his arms around her, to draw from him the strength necessary to get through the rest of the night.

Later they cut the cake, and another round of pictures was snapped. Riley was drawn into conversation with the owner of one of the horses he trained, and

Noelle slipped up behind Darcy and placed a sisterly arm around her shoulders.

"Come with me, friend. I want to hear all about the wedding to which I was not invited."

Darcy followed her outside and up the stairs behind the barn to the private office. They collapsed on the sofa, and Noelle kicked off her high heels. "Too bad you two couldn't have waited a few weeks until after Labor Day and the big race. I would have loved planning your wedding. We could have had a beautiful ceremony right here."

"It came up kind of unexpectedly," Darcy put in uneasily.

Noelle gave her a knowing look and patted her expanding girth. "I'm well versed in love and hormones. I just hope you two will be as happy as Brody and I have been."

Darcy opened her mouth to tell her best friend, now sister-in-law, that she was sure they would be. But the lie wouldn't come, and she burst into tears.

Noelle gathered Darcy in her arms, comforting her until the sobbing stopped. "What is it, honey? What's wrong?"

"It—it's all a lie. A big f-fat lie."

Noelle handed her a tissue. "What's a lie? I don't understand."

"How could you? I don't even understand. I can't believe I did this."

Noelle looked concerned. "Are you saying you made a mistake in marrying Riley? Maybe it's just nerves or something."

"No, it isn't," Darcy denied hotly. "I never should have gone through with it. I shouldn't have let him charm me into it."

"What are you talking about?" Noelle seemed at a loss to understand.

"He doesn't really love me," she sputtered wetly.

"Not love you? How can you think such a thing? I know you and Riley have been through a lot, but you shouldn't doubt his feelings. He's never stopped loving you."

"That's not why he married me. If I tell you something, do you swear not to repeat it?"

Noelle frowned. "Not even to Brody?"

"Definitely not to Brody."

Noelle hesitated only a moment. "Okay, I swear. I've been your friend a lot longer than I've been Brody's wife."

Darcy blew her nose and wiped her eyes. "Riley only married me to get custody of Jamaica and Tyler."

Noelle's eyes widened. "That kind of dishonesty doesn't sound like Riley."

"Oh, he was very honest about it. We made a deal."

"I don't believe it. I could tell by the look on his face when he made that toast that he meant every word he said."

"What he was really saying was that he was just grateful for the favor. You know Riley. He can make anyone believe anything. He's so concerned about the kids that he coerced me into marrying him so he could get permanent custody from Candi's sister, Marsha."

"Coerced, Darcy?"

"Okay," she conceded. "He persuaded me. They're giving Marsha a bad time, and she's having trouble

coping with them and her own children. But she feels
they'd be better off in a foster home than with a single
parent with Riley's history.''

"Uh-oh.''

"Uh-oh, is right. Saying foster home to Riley is like
waving a red flag in front of a bull. He and I made a
deal today, that's all. He'll help Mother and Cord fi-
nancially, pay off their bills and see to their needs.''

"And?'' Noelle prompted.

"I'll pretend to be Mrs. Riley Sawyer for six
months.''

Noelle gasped. "You mean you aren't really married? Goodness, what will all those people down there
think when they find out?''

"Calm down. You don't have to return the wedding
gifts. We got married all right.'' Darcy sighed and
fished a compact out of her purse. Repairing the rav-
ages of her crying jag, she explained. "It's all legal and
binding. He needs proof for the custody hearing or
something.''

Her friend eyed Darcy skeptically. "So where does
the pretending part come in?''

"You've heard the term marriage of convenience?''

"Only in old-fashioned romantic novels,'' Noelle
said. "Doesn't the penniless young aristocrat usually
agree to marry the nobleman so he can claim his right-
ful inheritance?''

"You've got it. I'm no aristocrat, but I'm pretty
close to penniless. And the inheritance Riley wants to
claim is named Tyler and Jamaica.''

"You can't be serious.'' Noelle stared at her in
disbelief. "Are you forgetting that I have witnessed the
hot chemistry between you two? It started the moment

you met and, if tonight was any indication, it hasn't burned out yet."

"Part of the deal was hands-off," Darcy admitted with a morose shrug. "It's to be a marriage in name only."

Noelle laughed and then clapped her hand over her mouth. "Sorry," she said at Darcy's dark look. "But surely you jest?"

"Believe it."

"I have a pretty vivid imagination, but I just can't visualize you and Riley sharing a house and sleeping in separate beds."

"Get used to the idea. Our relationship will be strictly platonic."

"Platonic?" Noelle shrieked, her delighted skepticism evident. "I'm sure you two will give a whole new meaning to the word."

Darcy glared at her friend before applying a light dusting of powder to her reddened nose. Satisfied with the results, she packed away her cosmetics. "Platonic," she insisted. "As in, no sex."

"I'd say it sounds more like a marriage of *inconvenience* for both of you. You two were made for each other."

"Physically maybe, and I don't deny that I still love him. But right now, that's how things stand between us. And I expect you to help me keep this horrible little skeleton in the closet, on threat of death and dismemberment."

"You have my word," Noelle said with mock solemnity. "I'd be laughed out of the county if I even suggested such a thing to anyone who knows either of you." She held up her right hand as if taking an oath.

"I do hereby swear and affirm that I will be an unwilling party to the scam Darcy Sawyer is trying to pull off. Amen."

"Good, because I promised Riley that everyone would think we were the most deliriously happy couple who ever exchanged vows."

"I have only one question. What happens at the end of six months?"

"Once he has custody, I go my way and he goes his."

Noelle rolled her eyes. "Oh, sure."

"Oh, sure what?"

"Nothing. But I'd bet a dollar to a hole in a doughnut that it never happens."

Darcy slumped on the couch. "I'll take that bet. You know how much I love doughnut holes."

"This reminds me of *It Happened One Night*. Clark Gable and Claudette Colbert tried platonic. They hung a blanket between their beds and called it the Wall of Jericho."

"So," Darcy prompted. She wasn't the old-movie buff that her friend was. "What happened?"

"It didn't work for them, either. You really should rent that movie sometime."

"I'll keep it in mind," Darcy said wryly. "I'm sure Riley and I will have a lot of time on our hands."

Noelle laughed. "Before this is all over, Darcy my girl, you are definitely gonna owe me some doughnut holes."

Chapter Three

It was after midnight before Darcy and Riley could slip away from the party. The ripe, warm night was bright with moonlight and heavy with promise. Its sweetness beckoned, and they walked home hand in hand. They followed a farm road that cut across a field of newly mown hay and through the stand of timber separating Riley's house from Brody's.

Sound carried easily on the country-quiet air, but there was little to disturb the stillness. The hum of cicadas, the call of a whippoorwill, the rustle of small creatures in the dew damp grass. It was a night made for secrets and soft sighs. A night made for lovers.

Darcy breathed deeply of the rich air and for the first time since she'd said, I do, the full impact of her situation settled on her. It stole upon her suddenly, surprisingly, this feeling that had eluded her throughout the long day. She was married.

This was her wedding night, and she was finally alone with her husband.

Riley seemed to sense her thoughts for he smiled and squeezed her hand. "We're home," he told her when they stepped onto the porch. He fumbled in the dark for the key to unlock the door, and Darcy stood beside him, feeling nervous and shy.

He had to try the familiar lock three times before it finally turned. He'd suggested walking home because he needed the extra time to get his galloping emotions under control. He thought the fresh air would clear his head. It hadn't worked. He was as shaky as a newborn foal.

He pushed the door and it swung open. Still under the spell of the evening, he turned to Darcy and swept one strong arm beneath her thighs. With the other arm behind her back, he lifted her up to his broad chest.

"What are you doing?" she squeaked. Her arms wound automatically around his neck.

"Carrying my bride over the threshold." Giving her a gentle squeeze, he strode through the door and kicked it shut behind him. "Welcome home, Mrs. Sawyer," he said in a husky voice, his head descending toward hers.

Darcy had no time to think before he kissed her lightly. She was even farther from rationality by the time the tip of his tongue grazed the outline of her lips. She gave herself up to the caress and tightened her arms around his neck.

Riley's tongue swept inside her mouth, hot, hungry and persuasive, as if her response had shattered his control. He released her legs, allowing her to slide down, but his hands caught her hips and pulled her to his hard body. He rocked against her in a lazy motion that gently matched the questing of his tongue, and she was captive to the sensations his kiss inspired. It was a feeling she remembered well from days gone by.

"Darcy, it's been too long," he murmured against her lips before he claimed them again.

She would have agreed with him, but she was too lost in feeling to speak. She moved in his arms, enjoying the feel of her breasts pressing into his chest.

Riley felt a moment of remorse for taking advantage of their old chemistry. But it was a brief one. He deepened the kiss and savored her urgent response. This part hadn't changed, he thought with elation. If anything it was better than ever.

When he released her, Darcy stood in the circle of his arms, her eyes closed dreamily, her heart beating wildly. "Why do I always feel shell-shocked when you kiss me?" she whispered, not expecting or needing an answer.

He moaned and buried his face in the graceful curve of her neck. His breathing was the only sound in the darkened room, and he held her tightly for several moments.

"That was to make up for bungling our wedding kiss. Now that I finally got it right, maybe I can live with myself," he explained with a slow smile. "I won't let it happen again. Unless you want it to."

"Under the circumstances," she said. "That wouldn't be a good idea."

"No, it wouldn't," he agreed. His reluctance to let it go at that was revealed by moonlight shining through the window. When he felt he could bear the separation, he stepped away and immediately tripped over something in his path.

"What was that?" Darcy asked.

"Your suitcases. One thing about Pete, he's always on the job." Peter was the hired hand who'd been dispatched to transport Darcy's things from her mother's house, where she'd been staying, to Riley's.

Darcy flipped on the light and the sudden illumination made them self-conscious again. She reached for a bag at the same time he did and they bumped heads.

"I'll carry it," he insisted.

"I can manage."

"You don't have to now. You have me to do it for you." Riley picked up the suitcase and lugged it into the bedroom.

Darcy followed and when she caught a glimpse of her kiss-swollen lips in the mirror, she felt the unwanted sting of tears. This was all wrong. The vows they'd spoken mocked her, that promise to love, honor and cherish. Forever. Or until the deadline was up.

All the fears and doubts that had plagued her during the past week marched through her mind in close-order drill. What kind of marriage would this be? The judge's pronouncement had made it legal. The celebration tonight had made it public. If only they shared the commitment to make it real.

Riley brought in the rest of her luggage and chattered inanely of things neither of them cared about. That wasn't like Riley. Was he feeling as miserable as she felt? Did he need assurance as much as she did? With a muttered excuse about making sure all the doors were locked, he hurried out of the room.

Even though there were less than six hours left until dawn, the night loomed long and lonely. It was her wedding night, and she would spend it alone. Her nerves unraveled more with each passing moment, and she paced around the room, which was decorated in subtle shades of mauve and gray. It took a moment for her to realize that Riley had installed her in the master bedroom.

The king-size bed was gone, and cherrywood twins stood in its place. They were covered by gray-and-white striped comforters that matched the drapes. A double dresser and mirror graced one wall, a highboy another. Soft light pooled beneath the fluted shade of a brass candlestick lamp on the nightstand between the beds.

She hoisted one of her bags onto the bed and began unpacking, not really seeing or thinking about the garments she unfolded.

The bedroom door opened suddenly and she whirled around. Riley's broad shoulders filled the wooden frame; the house beyond him was dark. He strode into the room and raised the north-facing window a few inches.

"I thought you'd prefer this bed," he told her, patting the comforter. "It's closest to the window, and I remember how you feel about fresh air at night."

"Thanks." What else did he remember? Was he also thinking how different things were between them the last time they shared this room? Did he remember the passionate way she had responded to him or the gentle way he had loved her?

He folded his arms across his chest and leaned against the dresser. His gaze skimmed her pale face, and wondered if her nerves were a result of memories of how they'd once shared much more than this room. His own nerves weren't much better off, and an uneasy smile twitched at the corners of his mouth. "I guess we should try to get some sleep."

"Yes, we should." Even though she agreed with him he made no move to go. Tearing her gaze from his, she added, "It's been a long day, and I'm tired. You'll be sleeping in Tyler's room, I suppose."

"I wasn't planning to."

She swallowed hard. It didn't take much imagination to figure out what he *was* planning. She'd been thinking along those same lines herself, but since that wasn't part of the deal, she willed such dangerous thoughts from her mind. "Surely you aren't thinking of sleeping in here?"

Riley raked back his hair. "We had this discussion on the phone, Darcy. This is a three-bedroom house. Jamaica will need one room. Tyler another. You agreed to share this one if I switched the king-size for two twins. I did that."

"I agreed to try to make this marriage look real to casual observers. To put on an act. Since the kids won't be here until Monday, I assumed we'd wait until then to move in together," she said lamely.

An eyebrow raised in amusement. "Why postpone the inevitable?"

"I don't know about you, but I didn't get much sleep last night. I think we'd rest better in separate rooms. Too much togetherness at this point would be a mistake."

Though he kept his mouth firm, his smile sparkled in his eyes. "Look, darlin', I promise not to pounce on you the minute you fall asleep. You can trust me that far, can't you?''

She looked down at the floor. "I didn't say I didn't trust you.''

This time there was no hiding the grin. "Maybe you don't trust yourself.''

"Did I say anything about trust?'' she demanded.

"No. But that's the problem and we both know it,'' he said softly. "That's what this whole thing is about. It's also why we need to do this now. You know what they say. Virtue is just the lack of temptation. How can I prove my good intentions if you lock yourself behind closed doors?''

"I guess it would be a good idea to develop a routine before the kids get here.'' Darcy frowned. "I must be more tired than I thought.''

"Why?''

"Because that makes sense to me.''

He crossed the space between them and placed his hands lightly on her shoulders. "I don't know about you, Darce,'' he said softly. "But I don't want to spend my wedding night all alone. It would mean a lot to me to know you're at least in the same room.''

Oh, Riley, she beseeched silently, why did we do this to ourselves? They had set up impossible limits that would demand inhuman strength to observe. But observe them she would for her own good. Besides, she owed it to him to live up to their bargain, to help him as she'd promised. If she couldn't keep a physical distance between them, she had to at least maintain an emotional one.

"I don't want to be alone, either. But how do we manage all this?" She waved her arm, a gesture that encompassed the whole room.

"All what?"

"Privacy."

"Well," he said, stalling. He shoved his hands deep into his pockets to keep from acting on a flood of impulses. Strong impulses that told him to touch her, kiss her, hold her. Love her. "We have our own bathroom in here and two big closets with a dressing room. That should give you plenty of privacy. If we plan it right, I won't have to see your underwear unless you want me to."

"I guess I can shower and change while you lock up at night and be in bed by the time you're finished."

"You can do all that in three or four minutes?" he asked incredulously. "It used to take you that long just to put lotion on your—"

"Riley!"

"What I meant was, this is no castle keep. We have a front door and a back door and a few windows. That's it."

She recognized the heavy-lidded look he gave her. She'd seen it plenty of times before. "What about tonight?" she asked nervously.

"What about it?"

"I need ten minutes alone."

What Riley needed was a cold shower. "You've got it." He strode through the door, carefully closing it behind him.

Darcy pulled a nightgown out of her suitcase. A white silk gown she did not remember packing. Wondering how it got there, she unfolded the long slinky garment, and a piece of paper fell on the bed.

She recognized the handwriting at once. Her mother's arthritis made it all but illegible. She read it, and a lump formed in her throat.

For my darling daughter on her wedding day.

Tears filled her eyes and overflowed as she read on.

I saw this in a shop window and knowing your penchant for tacky nightshirts, I decided it was the perfect gift. Wear it tonight and know that you have my wishes for a long and happy marriage.
                                    Love, Mother.

Darcy swiped the tears from her cheeks, refolded the note and quickly tucked it into one of her assigned drawers. When she'd told her mother she was marrying Riley, Ida had shed a few tears of her own.

"Don't think I'm not happy for you," she'd said. "If Riley is the man you want, then he is the man you should have."

Interpreting her mother's misgivings, Darcy had defended her decision. "He's not like Daddy. Riley's beating the alcoholism." She had wanted to share the reasons for the sudden marriage, but she'd kept quiet. The truth would only have worried her mother, and the lady didn't need any more worries.

Ida had hugged her close, stroking her hair as she had when Darcy was a little girl. "I hope he isn't too different from your father. Your daddy was a very loving man.''

Loving, but weak, Darcy had wanted to say. Riley was strong. When he wanted something, he got it. If only he wanted her and not just the advantages of marriage.

Darcy held the gown close to her chest and vacillated for a moment about whether or not to wear it. Time was running out, and sentiment won. She slung it over her shoulder, dashed into the bathroom, then ran back to her suitcase to hunt for her shower cap. She pulled a towel from the linen cabinet and jumped under the shower.

She gasped when the first shock of cold water pelted her skin, but its relentless chill was exactly what she needed to make her rush through what was normally a lengthy routine. She dried herself quickly and pulled the filmy nightgown over her head and down her still-damp body.

The sleeveless gown was gathered at the shoulders and fell into a deep V neckline that nearly dipped to her waist. The silky fabric hugged her curves, flaring around her hips to fall in graceful folds all the way to her feet.

She spent precious seconds staring at her reflection in the steamy mirror. The gown was certainly bridal looking, she realized. Too bad its allure would be wasted tonight.

The minutes ticked away as she creamed the makeup from her face and gave her tangled hair a quick once-over with the brush. Hurrying, she snatched up her belongings and tossed the whole caboodle into her closet to be dealt with in the morning.

Bolting breathlessly into the bedroom she dove into bed. Just in the nick of time, judging by the clock on the nightstand. She had thirty seconds to spare. She was tugging up the covers when Riley tapped lightly and walked in.

"What did you use, a stopwatch?" she asked.

"Do you need more time?" Despite his innocent tone, his gaze was captured by her silk-clad breasts heaving above the sheet she'd tucked in around her. Her hair was a riot of wayward curls, and her pretty face was scrubbed clean of artifice. God, she was beautiful. He wanted her so much the need was a physical ache.

"If there's anything you want," he told her, "just ask. Anything at all."

"No. I'm fine." She flopped back on the bed and turned her back to him before covering her head.

Riley watched her wiggle beneath the covers and headed straight for the restorative powers of cold water. Nothing would work better to assuage the feelings he had no business feeling right now. Except maybe a warm bed built for two.

The icy water dispelled those notions in a hurry. When he deemed himself sufficiently punished, he stepped out of the shower. As he vigorously towel dried his hair, he wondered if he should shave again. Deciding the effort would be pointless under the circumstances, he combed his hair and pulled on pajama bottoms purchased for the occasion.

He switched off the light and climbed into the narrow bed that was to be his prison for the next six months. No more than three feet separated him from the woman he loved, but it might as well have been three miles. Three light-years. "You can come out now," he told her. "It's safe."

Darcy didn't think she'd ever be safe again, but she relaxed against her pillow and sighed. "Good night, Riley."

"Good night." He thumped the pillow with his fist and turned over. What was so damned good about it?

A little later, Darcy groaned when she felt nature trying to lure her out of the cocoon she'd made for herself. Why hadn't she used the bathroom when she was in there? Always go before you leave home. It was a rule she'd learned as a toddler.

She tried to put mind over matter, willing herself to sleep, but it was no use. She would have to get up. Making as little noise as possible, she slipped out of bed. Feeling her way through the unfamiliar room, she tiptoed across the carpet in the dark.

She was on her way back when a sudden and deafening clamor shattered the still night. Startled, she tripped and fell backward onto Riley's bed.

"What the—" He bolted upright as Darcy tumbled down on top of him. "Darlin', does this mean what I hope it means?" he asked her.

Her reply was drowned out by another frightening peal of metal against metal, and she wrapped her arms around him in fear. The ear-splitting noise grew louder, until it seemed to surround them. It was as if the house were under siege by commandos armed with pots and pans and washboards.

Hesitating long enough to enjoy Darcy's weight on him, Riley peeled her arms from around his waist. In a deft motion, he rolled away, off the bed, and crouched on the floor near the window.

"Mr. and Mrs. Riley Sawyer!" hailed a laughing voice from outside. "You are hereby commanded to appear!" The voice was immediately joined by many others, until the chanting summons seemed to come from every direction.

"Who's there?" Riley bellowed, knowing full well that the disturber of his peace was Brody.

Darcy, assured that they weren't under imminent attack, peeked out the window. "Good grief," she exclaimed. "It's the whole darn reception party."

"Don't shoot," Noelle called. "We're friend, not foe."

"Damn." Riley found his slacks and slipped them on. One glance at Darcy, who looked like a wanton temptress, prompted him to advise her, "You'd better put on a robe or something, unless you want to greet our first guests in that getup."

"Surely they don't actually mean to come in?" she cried in distress as she flung open the closet.

"Oh, but they do. I'm pretty sure they mean to do a lot more than that, but we'll just have to wait and see."

"More?" Darcy screeched as she dug through her suitcases, searching for the caftan she knew was there somewhere.

Riley chuckled and tossed her the dark blue velour robe from the foot of his bed. "If I were you, I'd slip into this before things get out of hand."

Darcy pulled it on. "What are you talking about?"

"We're about to be the victims of what's known as an old-fashioned shivaree, darlin'."

"People don't do that anymore," she denied hotly. Looking at him uncertainly she whispered, "Do they?"

He grinned when the noise rose up again. "Judging by the sound of things, I'd say yes."

"But it's barbaric."

"It's also a much-cherished local custom."

From outside, Brody called, "Come on, open up, you two lovebirds. You have company." The members of the pot-and-pan orchestra picked up the tempo with renewed fervor.

Riley took Darcy by the hand and led her through the dark living room to the front door. The moment they stepped outside they were pulled apart. Despite their protests, the men led Riley to one pickup truck while the women escorted Darcy to a second.

Amid much teasing and backslapping, everyone piled into the vehicles. Brody called out, "Hey, Darcy!"

"What, Brody?"

"Riley's worried that you might be scared. No need to be. We just want to give you a night you won't forget."

Everyone laughed, including Darcy who was beginning to appreciate the company. Their friends' prank had taken her mind off the immediate problem of how to spend the night. "I'm fine."

"Then say goodbye to your husband, girl." Brody urged as the truck he was driving sped by.

"Goodbye, husband." Darcy saw Riley's frantic wave before he disappeared from sight.

The women sat on blankets in the back of the truck, and what followed was a wild ride over the rolling countryside. As they careered down a dirt road, excitement welled within Darcy. The night wind lifted her hair from her shoulders and whipped it around her face.

The laughing and joking passengers lolled against one another and held on tightly as the trucks rocked over a rough road that ran through a densely wooded area. After about twenty minutes, they came to an abrupt halt at what appeared to be an old abandoned cabin.

Noelle got out of the cab and leaned close to Darcy, speaking for the first time since the ride began. "I'm sorry. I tried to talk them out of this, but Brody wanted payback for a practical joke Riley played on him in Ruidoso."

"No problem," Darcy said with a giggle. "It's a strange way to have a party, but it's actually kind of fun." The unexpected companions had cured a bad case of wedding-night jitters and she was actually beginning to enjoy herself.

Noelle eyed her skeptically. "You're taking this rather well. Have you ever been in on a shivaree before?"

"No, but it all seems harmless enough."

"I hope you still think so an hour from now," Noelle said ominously.

"Why? What happens next?"

"Normally the bride and groom are kept apart for the wedding night."

A look of immense relief flooded Darcy's face. "Oh, thank goodness. I was really getting worried."

Noelle hesitated before continuing. "According to tradition, the groom is then gotten so intoxicated that his...uh...performance is impaired."

"No! They can't."

"Right. They can't. So that's why things had to be modified a little. Somebody had the bright idea of stranding you two in the cabin. Forced togetherness instead of separation."

"Oh, no." Panic-stricken, Darcy grabbed Noelle's arm. "We can't stay out here all night."

"Don't worry," Noelle whispered. "As soon as Brody falls asleep, I'll sneak back and take you home."

Darcy slumped. "Thanks a whole bunch."

"Cheer up," her friend advised her. "Believe it or not it could be worse."

"How?"

"In ancient times custom required witnesses to view the actual...uh...bedding. If you get my drift."

"I get it. Thank goodness we're living in such enlightened times as these," Darcy said sarcastically.

Joshing and hooting, the men carried Riley into the cabin, which Noelle explained was used by the Sawyer men and their friends as a hunting cabin during deer season. After much catcalling and laughter, they emerged one by one. Brody waved Riley's slacks and pajama bottoms aloft like banners.

At this unspoken signal, the men climbed into their truck and drove away. The women circled around Darcy and tugged at her gown and robe.

"Wait just a darn minute." Darcy clung fast to her clothing and protested that if this was a joke, she didn't think it funny anymore.

Noelle sighed and gave her friend a long-suffering look. The other women, who only hours ago toasted her future happiness, exhorted her to be a good sport and quickly confiscated her clothing.

Overwhelmed and unsure what she could do under the circumstances, Darcy stood in the dark, bare as the day she was born, as a soft night breeze kissed her skin. She couldn't remember the last time she'd been naked out of doors. Maybe never.

She was bewildered by the turn of events, but somewhere beneath the embarrassment and confusion was an unexpected feeling of arousal. Deciding that making a scene would only humiliate her, Darcy stood proudly inside the circle of women.

With the moonlight bathing her in its soft glow, she felt like some primitive woman being readied by the other females of her tribe for an ancient pagan ritual. Her man, strong and virile, awaited her in a sacred cave deep in a lush and fertile jungle.

Darcy laughed at her own wild fancy. Maybe being Rama the jungle maiden wasn't every woman's fantasy, but it would certainly do until something better came along.

"I really am sorry," Noelle whispered as she handed Darcy a battery-operated camp light. "Take this, just in case."

Darcy accepted the lantern, but did not switch it on. "Just in case what, Noelle? That I want to do a little reading tonight?"

When the other women stopped laughing, Noelle said, "Don't worry, it's so dark no one can see you. Keep the light off until we shut the door behind you."

"Right," Darcy mumbled. She slowly climbed the rickety wooden steps and entered the dark windowless cabin that was hardly more than a hut. She stepped inside, and the door was closed firmly behind her. She half expected to hear a bolt being shot home. She didn't.

She supposed she should be grateful that she wasn't locked in, but wasn't she? She was out here in the middle of pitch-dark nowhere without a stitch of clothes. Where could she go? In effect, she was a prisoner until Noelle returned to set her free. Only she wasn't alone, she had a dangerous cell mate.

Her brand-new husband was here. Somewhere.

Modesty prevented her from switching on the light. "Riley?" she called tentatively into a darkness so black it was beyond dark. There was one good thing about the dark—mice you couldn't see couldn't hurt you. "Riley?" she repeated a little louder. "Where are you? It's as black as the inside of a tar bucket in here."

"You have a light, don't you?" called a cheerful voice from across the small room. "Turn it on."

"I don't think so."

"Why not?" came the innocent question.

"You know darn well why not. I'm naked as a jay-bird."

"Me, too. Turn on the light."

"Riley!"

"Sorry. But it won't be anything I haven't seen before," he reminded her.

"Well, it's something you won't be seeing tonight."

"So what do you suggest?" he asked.

"I was hoping you might have an idea."

"I do. Want to hear it?"

Darcy didn't have to see his face to interpret the intent behind that remark. "No. What are we going to do?"

"Well, I can't do much of anything."

"Why not, pray tell?"

"I'm kinda tied up at the moment."

She thought she heard a muffled snicker. "Tied up?" she ventured.

"Yep."

She repressed a giggle. Was there no limit to how far Brody would go for a joke? "As in literally or figuratively?"

Riley was silent for several seconds. When it came, his answer was full of portent. "Guess."

Chapter Four

Darcy laughed out loud. "I'm afraid my imagination is not up to task. Maybe I'll turn on the light and check it out firsthand."

"Be my guest," Riley invited in a seductive voice. "But be warned. The light may not be the only thing turned on."

His provocative remark reminded Darcy of her state of undress, and she groped around hoping to find a blanket or some other covering. Finding nothing, she said in exasperation, "What kind of place is this?"

"A honeymoon cottage?" he suggested helpfully.

"Very funny." As her eyes adjusted to the darkness, she could make out vague shapes in the room. "Do you suppose they really plan to leave us here all night?"

"Or until someone remembers where we are. When the gang shivareed Brody and Noelle they took them to separate motel rooms and stole all their clothes, bedding, everything. It took the newlyweds several hours to figure out they were in adjoining rooms all along."

"I wasn't in on the shivaree, but I heard later that Brody was fit to be tied," Darcy put in.

"That's how I heard it. Now speaking of tied—how about giving me a hand over here?"

"Considering I can't see a thing, wouldn't that be a little risky?" she asked.

"There's always the light."

"No." She was adamant.

Riley sighed. "This is not the time for misplaced modesty, Darcy."

She stepped farther into the room, ready to explain that her modesty was not misplaced, when a familiar aroma filled her nostrils and made her stomach rumble. "Mmm, fried chicken. I'm hungry."

After a slight pause, Riley said in a husky voice, "So am I. Turn on the light so we can find the picnic basket I heard the men talking about."

"I can't."

"For Pete's sake, Darce. Why not?"

"Because we're . . . not dressed." Reluctant as she was, Darcy knew she'd have to switch on the lamp sooner or later. She couldn't very well stand around in the dark all night, like Lady Godiva looking for her horse. She ran her hand over the battery-powered lantern, measuring.

It would provide coverage if held strategically. And if she kept the beam focused properly, maybe it wouldn't reveal too much. She fluffed her long hair and made sure her chest was covered before sliding the button to the on position.

The small cabin was about what one would expect of a hunter's lair. The beam of light illuminated rough log walls decorated with old calendars and pictures torn from magazines. Magazines that were definitely not *Field and Stream*.

A rusting wood stove squatted in one corner, and the pile of logs beside it was draped with spiderwebs. A nicked table and four chairs, none of which matched, occupied another corner. Spotting a checkerboard with bottle caps for checkers open in the middle of the table, Darcy sighed. At least they'd have something to keep their hands busy.

All in all, the accommodations weren't what one would call impressive. At least that's what she thought until the light played across a set of rough-hewn bunk beds nailed onto the opposite wall. The top bunk, stripped down to the wooden slats, was of no interest.

But Darcy's pulse skidded and thumped at the sight of an equally stripped Riley spread-eagle on a bare mattress on the bottom bunk, his hands and legs secured to the bed frame with what appeared to be black chiffon scarves.

She rolled her eyes. *Nice touch, fellas.*

Riley had never been particularly fond of bondage, but the look on Darcy's face made the minor discomfort worthwhile. "Either have your way with me, wife, or close your mouth and untie me."

Darcy swallowed hard and quickly reclaimed her composure. "I think things would be less complicated if I left you like this until morning."

"That's easy for you to say," he put in dryly, "when it's not your circulation that's being impaired."

Genuinely concerned for him, Darcy quickly crossed the room. Setting the lantern down, she knelt on the floor beside the bed and stroked his hand. "Are you numb?"

Riley was disappointed. The dim light didn't reveal much—the flash of a tantalizingly rounded hip, the curve of a pale breast half-hidden behind swinging black hair, dark eyes liquid with emotion—but those teasing glimpses, coupled with the shock of Darcy's touch were enough to kick his hormones into overdrive.

Several seconds ticked by. "Only parts of me, darlin'."

Working on the knotted scarves, Darcy soon realized the bonds were mostly for show. Flimsily tied, they wouldn't have held a newborn kitten if it had truly desired to escape. The moment Riley's hands were free, she scooted back into the shadows.

"Your friends have a warped sense of humor," she said, "leaving us way out here without so much as a blanket."

His back to her, Riley untied his feet and swung them to the floor. "Lucky for us it's August, huh?"

She kept her eyes carefully averted from the raw masculinity on display. Even if he was her husband, they had an agreement. But that agreement had been made before she'd known about shivarees. "Lucky? How can you call anything about this awful night lucky?" she demanded from her new position behind the stove.

"Oh, I don't know. I could think of worse scenarios." Riley ached with the need to pull Darcy from the shadows and clasp her to him. To feel the sleek length of her lovely body pressed against his. To taste the sweet honey of her kisses. "Here."

"Here what?" she asked suspiciously.

He held out a diaphanous pile of black chiffon. "There's enough material here to protect your modesty. See what you can make of these."

She eyed the gauzy scarves doubtfully. They *were* large and square. Unfortunately they were also nearly transparent. But they were definitely better than nothing. "Throw them to me."

Riley feigned offense. "If I didn't know better, I'd think you didn't trust me." He tossed her the scarves, keeping two with which he fashioned a garment that was a cross between a diaper and a sarong. Not exactly the latest in ranchwear, but if it was good enough for South Seas islanders, it was good enough for him.

"How are you doing over there?" he called into the darkness. Aside from a few shuffling sounds, one or two sighs of frustration and the soft rip of fabric, all was silent in Darcy's corner.

"I'm doing just fine considering what I have to work with, thank you." She tied the last knot and stepped out of the gloom. Riley had propped the lantern up on the table, and the beam illuminated a circle about five feet in diameter. He was seated in one of the chairs with only his broad chest visible above the table. The picnic basket was before him.

He tried to remain unmoved as Darcy approached, but such detachment eluded him. With considerable skill she had rendered the two scarves into an outfit straight out of a lonely man's fantasy. She had folded one to a nearly opaque stage and tied it around her chest like a bikini top, leaving the unfolded part to hang down her midriff.

The other she had torn into two unequal strips. Rolled and tied low on her hips, one piece formed a belt, the other was folded and slipped between her legs to tuck in front and back. While it provided decent coverage, the overall effect of the outfit was far more exciting than complete nudity, and Riley let out the breath he'd been holding.

"Now that we're properly dressed, would you like something to eat?" he asked in as normal a voice as he could manage.

"I'd like to get out of here."

"Get used to it, darlin'—we're here for the duration."

Feeling embarrassed and self-conscious, Darcy slid into the chair opposite him. She knew she had more covering than many of the women she'd seen at the pool this summer, but the feeling of exposure was unnerving. Or perhaps it was the feeling of sensual arousal that troubled her so much.

"I still say the whole shivaree thing is cruel and unjust punishment," she said.

"My friends thought they were being kind. In the old days they would've kept us separated all night long. Now that's punishment."

She folded her arms across her chest. "I would've preferred that to being stripped and abandoned."

"Most newly married couples wouldn't find our fate so objectionable," he pointed out. In an effort to retrain his errant thoughts, he fished around in the basket. However, Darcy's nearness only increased his need. "Let's see what they packed in here."

He plucked a note from inside the basket and read it aloud. "'Just a little something to keep your strength up.' It's from the guys who work for us," he explained.

"How thoughtful," she grumbled when he pulled out a plastic bag. "Two measley little chicken breasts."

"Probably their idea of a joke."

"Not a very funny one, but then none of this is exactly hilarious," she said.

He held up a small vial. "Stress vitamins, I believe. Do you want one?"

"I'll pass."

He retrieved the next item. "A can of whipped cream." His voice held a note of innocent wonder that wasn't quite genuine. "I wonder what we're supposed to do with this?"

Darcy's cheeks flamed and she carefully avoided looking at her husband. "Maybe there's a strawberry shortcake in there somewhere."

"No such luck." He plucked the lid off a plastic container. "This must be some kind of first-aid kit. Petroleum jelly and—"

She snatched it from him and thrust it out of sight. "Don't open anything else," she said peevishly.

"But, darlin', it's a wedding gift. How can we fill out the thank-you card if we don't see what's inside?" He held the last container out of her reach and pried off the lid.

She turned her head away. "I refuse to look."

He laughed. "You're missing a real treat. What if I just tell you about it?"

"No." She covered her ears.

"Does that mean I get to eat all the cookies myself?"

"Cookies!" she exclaimed. "Give me that."

They sipped from cans of ginger ale and ate their chocolate-chip treats in uncomfortable silence. While packing away leftovers, both pointedly ignored the other "gifts."

Riley set the basket on the floor. "That killed twenty whole minutes. What do we do now?"

She shrugged and got to her feet. She didn't have any ideas, but it wasn't wise to let Riley's imagination run amuck. "We could play checkers," she suggested as she paced around the small cabin.

"We could do that, but it doesn't sound like much fun."

"I'm surprised your so-called friends didn't consider the entertainment aspect when they packed the basket."

"They probably assumed we'd think of something." He moved to the bunks and reclined on the lower one, watching her.

She sensed his eyes on her and felt naked all over again. "What are you looking at?"

"You."

"Why?"

"You're my wife. Aren't I at least allowed to look? I thought looking was covered under marital rights or something."

Her throat tightened up when she started thinking about what other rights he might have. And what rights she had as his wife. "Sit up," she commanded.

He didn't. "I'm tired."

"So am I."

He scooted over on the narrow bed to make room for her. "I'm willing to share."

"You must be kidding!"

"Nope," he said convincingly as he switched off the lamp. "We're both adults and we can handle this in a mature manner."

"All right." She hugged herself and fought the desire to confess that she wanted him to handle *her* in a mature manner. It was with misgivings that she scooted onto the bunk, wondering if she would survive the tension building to a fatal level inside her.

No longer sleepy, he turned his head in her direction and was careful not to touch her. "Comfy?"

She clutched her hands together to keep her arm from dangling off the bed. "No. It's too crowded."

He smiled and turned on his side, facing her. He lifted her shoulders and slid his arm beneath her neck, pulling her toward him.

"Riley..."

"There, that's better," he said as he closed his eyes. He clenched his teeth in an effort to hold on to his ravaged self-control.

More aware of him than she'd ever been before, Darcy squirmed and tried to put a bit more distance between them. Her heart was beating so crazily she feared he could feel it.

"This platonic stuff isn't easy for me, so be still, darlin'," he growled. "Unless you want to spend the rest of the night doing something besides sleeping."

She stiffened and for a moment was tempted to give into the painful need she felt. But making love to Riley would only complicate things and make it harder to leave when the time came. God only knew how difficult that would be.

Before long, his even breathing told her he was asleep. Willing herself to relax, one tense muscle at a time, she finally drifted into a dream.

A sweet dream of Riley holding her in his arms. Riley kissing her. His soft lips gently deliberated over hers; his questing tongue found what it sought. A dream in which Riley kissed away the hurts of the past, erased the painful memories, obliterated yesterday to make room for tomorrow. Darcy's senses buzzed when his tongue trailed slowly over her lips, when his hands skimmed over her back and hips.

"You're incredibly beautiful," he murmured in a voice too real to be a dream. Stroking the hair from her face, he kissed her again. His mouth wandered over the curve of her throat, then lower to possess the lushness of her breasts. His hands were everywhere and she was burning for him.

"Riley..." In the dream, Darcy tried to tell him how much she'd missed him, how happy she was that they were together at last, but someone was knocking on the door and calling their names.

"Darcy? Riley? It's me, Noelle."

"Darlin'?" Riley asked softly, and Darcy opened her eyes in alarm.

"Oh!" Riley was leaning over her, and she couldn't recall when the dream had ended. "I was asleep, dreaming..."

"Yeah, I agree. It was quite a dream," he whispered.

There was another pounding on the door and then Noelle called out, "Hey, do you guys still want a ride home?"

"Coming." Darcy shot off the bed and straightened her makeshift bikini. She groped in the darkness for the lamp, and Riley opened the door a crack. A feminine hand appeared at the opening and thrust their clothing inside.

Suddenly embarrassed, Darcy and Riley dressed quickly and stepped out onto the porch. Noelle was waiting by the truck.

"Hurry. I want to get back before Brody wakes up and finds me gone. I don't want to lie to him."

Riley nodded. "We wouldn't ask you to do that."

"I told Noelle . . . everything," Darcy explained.

"I'm sorry I couldn't get here sooner, but Brody wouldn't hear of me spoiling what he felt was romantic fun."

The ride home was accomplished in silence, giving Darcy plenty of time to think. How much of her dream had been real? Her responses certainly had been. How could she face him after such wanton behavior? How could they go on living this lie?

It took all the composure Riley could muster to keep quiet. It was gratifying to know that Darcy wasn't immune to him, after all. He'd woken from his doze at the first touch of her hand on his chest. When he'd taken her into his arms, he'd thought she was awake because her mouth had opened so sweetly to him.

He'd felt her response and there was no mistaking her passion. Six months. A lot could happen in that length of time, especially if he hurried it along. He smiled a secret smile. Not even the realization that Darcy had been dreaming when she kissed him could burst his happy bubble.

Chapter Five

I wish I could be here when the children arrive,"
Darcy fretted. "But I can't take Monday off—we're
much too busy at the bank."

Riley scooped up her briefcase, umbrella and lunch
and dumped them into her arms. "I know you can't
ask for time off when you're working out a notice. I'll
explain to Jamaica and Tyler, and they'll understand." Smoothing her scrunched-up brow with a light
touch, he reminded her, "It's just for two more weeks.
Then you'll be here full-time."

Having had a taste of independence in Nashville,
Darcy hadn't really wanted to return to the grind of a
nine-to-five job. She'd done so to help support her
family, but now that she was married to Riley, money
was the least of her worries. Not only would he and the
children need her at home, but by giving up her job she
would be able to devote more time to her music.

Though she had managed to keep busy, Darcy had done a lot of thinking over the weekend. If she wasn't going to be Riley's wife in every sense of the word, it was wrong to let him support her indefinitely. She'd already sold two pieces of work and hoped that the income from those and future sales would provide a comfortable living later.

Later. That's how she thought of the future, but it really translated into the time when she would no longer be with Riley. They were careful not to talk about it, but Darcy knew it had to be considered. She had to have a contingency plan. Riley's generous promise to assume her mother's medical expenses and subsidize Cord's education had given her a second chance at her dream, but she couldn't accept his help forever.

She would allow herself these six months to succeed in her chosen field. If she failed she would abandon it for good and return to the business world and never look back. Considering that some writers struggled for years before they made it, she knew she wasn't giving herself much time. But it was all she could afford.

She smiled and took a last look around the house. Despite the rain and gloom outside, she had cranked up the wooden miniblinds in the living room to admit whatever light the day might offer. A large fan whirred softly from the beamed ceiling. The plush beige carpeting still bore the tracks of her vacuum cleaner, and a clutch of newly purchased child-rearing books were lined up neatly on the shelves beside the fireplace.

The overstuffed couch was plump with throw pillows and the oak tabletops gleamed with polish. In one corner was her prized cherrywood spinet, newly transported from her mother's house. The piano and the guitar propped against it, awaited serious songwriting sessions.

Darcy hadn't had time to add many feminine touches to the masculine decor but she and Riley had spent all day Saturday cleaning and making sure everything was perfect for the children's arrival. Their rooms were spotless, the beds made up with fresh linen. At her urging, Riley had hauled bookcases from the den into the children's bedrooms so that Tyler and Jamaica would have ample space for their things. She wanted them to feel welcome. On Sunday, she and Riley had driven into town to shop, and the shiny kitchen was stocked with all the foods children were supposed to love. This morning, she'd gotten up an hour early to prepare a casserole for tonight's dinner and it was in the fridge, ready for the microwave.

All seemed to be in order. Darcy started for the door, then paused. If everything was so perfect, why was she reluctant to leave? And why was her stomach tied up in knots? "Are you sure...?" she began.

"I'm very sure." Riley opened the door and eased her out into the gentle rainfall. Popping open her umbrella he urged, "Go. It's time for you to fling yourself on the altar of commerce."

"I'll try to come home early," she insisted.

He smiled at her self-inflicted anxiety. He'd always known she was a woman who cared deeply about others, but this was a new twist. Who would have thought his Darcy was such a mother hen? He kissed her lightly on the cheek. "We'll all be here, darlin'. Waiting for you to come home to us."

Home, Darcy mused as she drove into the city. It had a nice ring to it.

All morning she sat at her desk fighting the temptation to call and check on how things were going. By lunchtime, she could resist no longer and phoned from the break room. No answer. It was too soon to worry, she told herself. It would take Riley a while to drive the sixty-odd miles to the children's aunt's house in Perry. Then he'd have to load up their things and drive back. They had probably stopped for lunch along the way, as well.

Around three o'clock her boss stopped by her desk and asked her to volunteer to stay an extra hour and finish up some work. Given no choice in the matter, she picked up the phone again to advise Riley of the change in plans.

The phone rang several times before an unfamiliar and somewhat sullen adolescent voice answered. "Sawyer residence."

"Hello, is this Jamaica?"

"Yeah."

"This is Darcy."

"Yeah?"

The "so what?" obviously got lost somewhere along the line so Darcy tried again. "How was the trip?" She didn't have much experience making small talk with thirteen-year-olds. Especially a thirteen-year-old with an attitude.

"Bor-r-ring."

Strike one. Darcy knew the children had problems, but she had hoped they'd meet her halfway. "I'm really happy you and Tyler are going to live with us." She should establish that up front. Dr. Bradley, the family therapist she and Riley had consulted last week, had stressed the importance of making the children feel welcome in their new home.

"I'll bet."

Okay, so she's not going to help me, Darcy thought. But with or without the children's cooperation, she was determined to make this work. "May I speak to Riley, please?"

"Not unless you're telepathic."

Darcy slowly counted to five. When she spoke, her voice was tight but pleasantly polite. "What do you mean, Jamaica?"

"He's not here."

Eavesdroppers would have been awed by Darcy's carefully maintained cool. "Where is he, Jamaica?"

"I don't know."

Since Brody was in Ruidoso, Billy Sixkiller had agreed to cover for Riley at the stables so Riley could stick close to home until Darcy's notice was worked out. "Did he say when he would be back?"

"Not exactly."

This was getting her nowhere. If Jamaica's behavior was any indication of the fun times ahead, it was going to be a long six months. "Will you see that he gets a message?"

"Okay, shoot."

Don't tempt me, kid. "Shall I wait while you get a pen and paper?"

"What for?"

"To write down the message, dear."

"You need it in writing?"

"Never mind. Just tell Riley when he gets in that I'll be stuck here until at least six o'clock. He's expecting me home early, so it's important he knows the plan has changed."

"Gotcha." The line went dead.

Darcy rubbed her temples. What had she gotten herself into? Oh, she liked children well enough, but she didn't understand them. Her own mother's advice had been to remember that kids did not think or act like miniature adults. But Ida had not given her a clue as to what made them tick. There was nothing like going into a game ignorant of the rules.

The knot in her stomach tightened when she admitted to herself that she knew absolutely zilch about being a mother. Or about being a stepmother, if in fact that was what she was supposed to be. All she knew about stepmothers came from fairy tales. They were invariably jealous, selfish, wicked and cruel. They abandoned their stepchildren in forests, fed them poisoned apples and made them sleep among the cinders. All in all, not a very lofty role to aspire to.

Riley's job was clearer—he'd been the children's stepfather for five years and had already established his authority. He had insight into their personalities. He had experience. What did she have? Five hundred years of bad press to live down.

According to their aunt, Tyler and Jamaica hadn't adjusted well to their mother's death, but at least the move to Cimarron wouldn't be traumatic for them. They'd lived there before and knew it well. They were moving back into their old rooms, slipping back into their old places.

The fact was, Darcy realized, she was the interloper. The stranger who'd have to carve out a place for herself and then fight to keep it. She'd sought professional advice and received a wealth of psychological double-talk, but no real answers. Dr. Bradley advised a wait-and-see approach. If the children were willing to accept her first as a friend, she might then earn their trust and eventually their love. Recalling her conversation with Jamaica, she figured the likelihood of that happening could be summed up in two words.

Fat chance.

The sun didn't find its way out from behind the gray clouds all day, and Darcy's mood grew as gloomy as the weather. By six-thirty, the uncertainty she'd experienced when the day was new had developed into full-fledged paranoia.

She was not equipped to be a parent. She couldn't even keep a philodendron alive. Noelle, who was a natural, nurturing mother, made it look easy, but Darcy knew the task was thankless under the best circumstances.

What little she knew of these two children had endeared them to her, but how could she be expected to step into their lives and take responsibility for their happiness?

The potential for disaster was mind-boggling.

When she arrived home, Darcy shored up her faltering self-esteem and made sure her face bore a happy smile before opening the front door. It was a wise tactical maneuver, for the sight that greeted her would have made even a seasoned mom's blood run cold.

The living room looked as if it had been treated to the indiscriminate attentions of a team of well-trained, but manic, baboon commandos. Pillows, toys, books, clothes and games were scattered randomly around the room. Every horizontal surface was cluttered with the remains of what could only have been a snacking marathon, and a trail of muddy footprints tracked across the carpet.

Suffering from shock, it took Darcy a few minutes to realize that nothing even remotely human moved in the debris. A rock video blared on the unwatched television set, and from a cage atop the spinet came the raucous cries of two small parakeets who were obviously not happy to be there.

She approached the cage cautiously and groaned when she saw the seed hulls and bird droppings littering the piano's shiny surface. With a grimace of disgust, she plucked up the cage and deposited it on a newspaper in the corner.

Deciding such total destruction could only have occurred during a crime wave, Darcy moved warily into the kitchen, half expecting to find the lifeless bodies of Riley and the children.

What she found was almost as shocking. Cabinet doors gaped open, the contents obviously ransacked. A gallon jug of milk, now warm, stood on the breakfast bar. She gasped when she spotted a shockingly bloodlike stain spreading over the white countertop, but closer inspection revealed cherry fruit-drink making gone awry. The sink overflowed with dirty dishes and a rank odor permeated the air. Darcy traced the stink to a half-empty can of dog food on the windowsill.

Dog food? They didn't own a dog.

She was still assessing the damage when the back door blew open, and Riley swept in.

"Well, it's about time you got home," he said. Heedless of the waxed floor, he shook the rain from his hat. A dark look clouded Darcy's face, and he realized his was not a greeting guaranteed to win points today.

"Me? Where in tarnation have you been?"

"I had to go out to the racetrack for a while."

"A while?" she insisted.

"All right, it was longer than a while. I assumed you'd be home early like you said, so I left the kids here."

"I called to tell you I'd be late. Didn't you get my message?"

"No, I did not."

"I forgot."

Darcy and Riley turned as one when a voice spoke behind them. Jamaica Brill stood in the doorway, one slim hip cocked defiantly. She was dressed in a ragged pair of jeans and a Rolling Stones T-shirt. The red tongue thrusting through the big red lips on her shirt-front seemed to express a philosophy all its own. She wore a set of stereo headphones clamped over her ears and a testy look on her heavily made-up face.

Darcy could only stare at the thick pancake foundation, the equally thick layer of white highlighting cream that circled her eyes and the inexpertly applied blue shadow that smudged her lids into bruises. The child's long eyelashes were formed into spikes by neon-blue mascara and her lips were outlined and painted with two shades of blood-red lipstick.

Darcy wasn't sure what look Jamaica was striving for, but what she'd achieved was "baby owl loses the brawl." Fighting the urge to sit on the child and scrub her face with industrial strength cold cream, Darcy said nothing. If Jamaica sensed Darcy's shock, she didn't show it. In fact, she blew a big pink bubble with her chewing gum, the picture of teenage boredom.

Riley spoke up. "You forgot to give me Darcy's message? Is that what you're saying, Jamaica?" The counselor had stressed the importance of active listening in parent-child communication, and the books the man had recommended supported that technique.

"Yeah." She blew another bubble, then popped it back into her mouth with a long purple fingernail.

Pausing long enough to form his next comment into a nonaccusatory message as the books suggested, Riley said, "It upsets me when I don't know what's going on."

"So sue me." Jamaica spun on her heel and headed down the hall toward her room.

Riley took a good look at the kitchen for the first time and glanced questioningly at Darcy. "What happened in here?"

In an effort to safety valve her anger, she started throwing dishes into the dishwasher. Better a few broken plates than a couple of kids' necks, she reasoned. "I don't know exactly, but I do have a theory. I've ruled out vile, wanton vandalism and am up to act of God. You know, tornado, typhoon, earthquake. That sort of thing."

"I guess the kids made kind of a mess."

"Mess? That's what you call this?" She waved her hand around the room and lowered her voice. "Starving sharks in a feeding frenzy make a mess. This house qualifies for disaster relief."

"Is the living room this bad?" Riley moved to help her clean up.

"Oh, no."

"That's a relief."

"It's worse! There's junk everywhere, mud on the carpet and bird poop on my piano!"

"Oh, yeah, I forgot to tell you the kids have pets." Riley swallowed hard and waited for her reaction.

"I don't do pets, Riley." She grabbed the dog food can off the windowsill. "And I especially don't do dogs." She flung the can into the trash.

As if an offstage director had yelled, "Cue the dog!" a small hairy mutt scuttled into the kitchen, its claws clicking on the tile floor. Close behind him was Tyler Brill, age nine and three-quarters.

"Hi, Riley. Hi, Darcy." The little boy was dressed in a pair of baggy shorts and a purple T-shirt. His blond hair was cut in an appealingly shaggy style, and his wide brown eyes looked at the adults expectantly. His gap-toothed grin warmed Darcy's chilly heart, and she smiled back despite her anger.

"Hi, Tyler. How're you doin'?"

"Great. I'm glad I'm here."

"So are we, pardner," Riley told him.

"Who's your friend?" Darcy asked as she eyed the scruffy-looking dog with distaste. The thing probably had fleas that he would generously share with the whole family.

"This is Beany. He's my buddy." Tyler knelt on the floor and ruffled the shaggy brown fur. Beany responded by licking him full in the face.

"Ooooh, don't let him do that." Darcy's horror made her speak without thinking. She liked animals in zoos, on farms, in woods. What would America be without the buffalo that roamed and the deer and the antelope that played? She just didn't share the widely held belief that furry, feathered and/or scaly critters belonged under the same roof with human beings.

"How come?" Tyler asked innocently.

Darcy mumbled something about germs and turned back to her cleanup.

Riley found himself in the role of peacemaker. "It's a proven fact that a dog's mouth has fewer germs than a person's."

"That's nice to know, Riley," Darcy told him with false brightness. "The next time you feel the need for a kiss coming on, maybe Beany will oblige you."

Riley took Tyler aside and after speaking to him in a low voice the boy bounded out of the room. Beany, barking and wheezing, followed him.

"I couldn't ask Tyler to give up the dog," Riley explained. "He took Candi's death hard, and Beany means a lot to him."

"I understand." Darcy scrubbed furiously at the cherry drink stain, angry with herself for begrudging the poor kid his dog. If she'd known what to expect maybe she would have handled it better.

"Then you don't mind?"

"It's your house, Riley, do whatever you want."

He turned her to face him. "No, Darcy, it's *our* house." He wrapped his arms around her and pulled her close. "Good or bad, we're in this together." He tipped up her chin and added, "For better or worse, remember?"

Darcy felt the kiss coming, so powerful was the magnetism of Riley's touch. Despite her remarks about

Beany, her lips parted expectantly and her eyelids fluttered down. One of Riley's special kisses could make her forget kids, dogs, even bird poop. It could make the sun shine on a rainy day. It could fill her with hope.

But it didn't come. Before anything truly magnificent transpired, Jamaica called from the doorway. "Yeah, Riley? Ty said you wanted to talk to me."

Expressing his frustration with a noisy sigh, Riley grinned at Darcy and relinquished her from his embrace. Beckoning his stepdaughter into the living room, the two disappeared.

Darcy put the kitchen to rights and popped the chicken casserole into the microwave oven. While it was cooking, she stirred up a batch of blueberry muffins from a mix and tossed a salad. She wasn't the most experienced cook in the world, but she could put a meal together fast. According to Noelle, speed was more important than skill where kids were concerned.

She spooned instant pudding into parfait glasses and topped them with canned whipped cream from the wedding-night basket. At least the hands would have the gratification of knowing their gift had been put to good—if not the intended—use.

She planned a lovely get-acquainted meal in the formal dining room and had laid out her nice linen placemats and napkins the night before. She was taking flatware from the drawer when Riley came in and set up a small portable television set on the breakfast counter.

"What's that for?" she asked.

"The kids' favorite show is coming on in a few minutes so I told them they could watch in here while we eat."

She stared at him, flabbergasted. One thing her mother had insisted on when she was growing up was family dinner. It was a time to talk to one another, to solve problems and share joys. In the Durant household the dinner hour was sacrosanct. The family had endured strife that would have torn others apart, and Darcy firmly believed that her mother's insistence on togetherness had contributed to its strength.

"You're kidding, right?"

Riley wasn't. "They straightened the living room and I cleaned up the mud. Everything's spick-and-span in there—not a bird dropping in sight."

"That's hardly the point."

"There's no harm in letting them watch their program," he said without conviction.

She bit back a sharp reply when she saw his face. God, he was as unsure about all this as she was. The counselor had told them to set limits, but not to be inflexible. To make rules, but to be willing to bend them. To offer guidance, but to let the children make their own decisions. What was all that supposed to mean? Plan a nice sit-down family meal, but end up gobbling it in front of the TV? She couldn't really blame Riley. His primary goal was to make the kids feel at home, to ease the transition. Even if it went against everything she believed in.

"Okay." She plopped the salad bowl on the bar and flipped the muffins into a napkin-lined basket. "Tell the little dears to wash their hands and come to the table, er, counter."

Riley smiled gratefully and hustled off.

* * *

A screeching automobile chase accompanied the salad course. Jamaica passed, saying she couldn't possibly eat green stuff without her mother's homemade dressing.

She also refused the main dish with the announcement that eating poultry was like walking through a salmonella mine field. Nor would she eat muffins from a mix. Didn't Darcy know how much deadly cholesterol they contained?

After politely thanking Jamaica for the nutrition update, Darcy concentrated on just getting through the meal.

In spirit, Tyler was perfectly willing to eat his dinner, but the flesh was weak and he complained of an upset stomach. Riley was worried that it might be serious, but Darcy was convinced the pain was the result of too many snacks and sugary soft drinks.

"I think all he needs is antacid and rest," Darcy said.

"You *think*?" Jamaica asked archly. "Don't you know?"

"I'm fairly certain," Darcy said through clenched teeth.

Jamaica tossed her head dismissively. "Mom would have known exactly what to do. But how would you know? You're nobody's mother, are you?"

Darcy sat quietly, counting, and keeping a lid on her anger. No, she wasn't anyone's mother, and the way things were going she wasn't likely to be.

Jamaica obviously had no dietary restrictions against pudding parfaits and licked the last of the goo from her fingers before flouncing out of the room.

Riley dosed Tyler with the medicine and sent him to the shower. A few minutes later, he got a call from the barns requesting his immediate presence. On his way out, he put his arm around Darcy encouragingly.

"Don't let Jamaica get to you. Her mother never made anything from scratch in her life, including salad dressing. And about that deal with Tyler. Candi was no Florence Nightingale. She probably would have phoned a sitter and gone out to dinner."

"Good idea. I'll keep that in mind for the next time," Darcy said morosely.

"Just take one day at a time. It's going to be all right," he assured her with a quick peck.

"Says who?"

"Says me." This time he held her face between his hands and kissed her deeply. "For better or worse. Don't forget."

After the door shut behind him, Darcy rested her head in her hands. With any luck at all, she'd already seen the worst.

Chapter Six

Although it defied credibility, breakfast was an even bigger disaster than dinner. Riley offered to cook while Darcy got ready for work, but coffee was the only thing he could make with any success. Hurrying through her morning routine she took over for him, but in her haste the eggs were overcooked, the bacon undercooked and the toast black. Riley scraped it and jokingly called it cajun style.

Tyler, whose appetite had survived the night, didn't seem to mind the less than perfect fare and ate with the enthusiasm of a growing boy. Jamaica, completely and devastatingly made-up at seven in the morning, complained about having to get up so early to eat a meal her mother had never held in high regard.

"Breakfast is the most important meal of the day," Darcy told her before she gulped down a cup of hot coffee. She wasn't about to admit that coffee was usually the extent of her morning meal. The strong brew was sure to completely blow out her already frazzled nerves, but what the heck. She needed it.

The girl poked at her bacon and eggs and remarked that *this* kind of breakfast was a major contributor to arteriosclerosis and early heart attack.

"I'm sorry, Jamaica," Darcy said, her composure sorely tested. "It will take me time to get used to a new routine. However, if you will please advise me of your preferences, I will certainly try to accommodate your tastes in the future." The girl gave her a glare for her trouble.

Riley was not blind to the conflict between Jamaica and Darcy, but he couldn't understand it. Darcy had gone out of her way to be nice to the girl, so why was Jamaica acting like such a little brat? Such unarmed combat was hard on the nerves this early in the morning, so he attempted to open up new avenues of communication. "How come you know so much about nutrition, Jamaica?"

"I don't know," came her typical nonresponse.

"She's a whatdyacallit? A hippo...hypo... hypodermiac," Tyler offered. "Every time she hears about some food causing cancer or something she thinks she's gonna croak." He clutched his neck with his hands, stuck out his tongue and crossed his eyes.

"I do not," Jamaica denied hotly. "You're such a dork, Tyler."

"Look who's talking, zombie face."

Before Riley could make a move to stop her, Jamaica used her fork to flip a rubbery piece of fried egg into her brother's face. His howl of outrage sparked

Beany into a bout of high-pitched barking that threatened all the ear drums in a five-mile radius. When the barking initiated shrill squawking from the budgies, Darcy finally understood the meaning of the phrase silence is golden. She would gladly give a week's pay for five minutes of silence right now.

Not to be outdone, Tyler retaliated with a glob of grape jelly that landed square in the middle of Jamaica's forehead. In Darcy's opinion, it blended right in with the rest of her makeup in both color and texture.

"Hang on, you two." Riley raised his voice above the din. "I don't know what you did in your old home, but in this house we eat our food. We do not use it to inflict pain."

Jamaica wiped off the jelly and glared at her stepfather then Darcy. "Oh, yeah? Darcy does."

"What?" A hundred counseling sessions could not have kept the screech out of Darcy's one-word question.

"Now everyone just calm down." Riley stalled for time, hoping he could remember what the parenting books said about sibling rivalry. Needing to release the tension building inside him, he snapped, "Beany! For Pete's sake, shut up!"

Beany tucked his tail and slunk out of the room. Tyler burst into tears. "You don't have to yell at him. He's just a little dog." The boy stumbled to his feet, knocked his chair over in the process and fled to his room.

"Cool move, slick," Jamaica told Riley with a smug grin.

His eyes widened in surprise, and he forgot all about parenting books. "Don't you dare speak to me in that tone of voice, young lady."

"You're not my father."

"Maybe not. But I'm the closest you'll ever get. Now apologize and go to your room."

"Sorry," she flung over her shoulder as she left.

It was the most insincere apology Darcy had ever heard. As she waited quietly for her husband's reaction, she couldn't help thinking it was about time he was on the receiving end of Jamaica's caustic tongue.

"What did I do wrong?" he asked her, bewilderment in every word.

She considered how much he could take in one swallow. He was new at this; maybe she should just start with the biggies. "I think your first mistake was thinking you could turn us into the smiling family on the breakfast-cereal commercials overnight."

"They're not bad kids," he said adamantly, more to reassure himself than her.

"No, Riley, they're not bad kids."

"This is as hard on them as it is for us."

"I'm sure it is." She got up and walked around the table to stand behind him. She leaned down and wrapped her arms around his neck. "They're not bad kids. But they're sad and scared kids. They're afraid of loving and losing again."

"They haven't even been here twenty-four hours and already they're driving me nuts," he admitted sadly.

"Me, too."

"Maybe it's my fault. Maybe I'm not cut out to be a father."

Darcy hugged him, and his nearness gave her strength. He had reassured her when she was down, now it was her turn. "I'm no expert but my guess is that if only qualified people had been allowed to be parents, the human race would have become extinct a long time ago."

He laughed, and the sound of it made Darcy's day. "Maybe you're right."

"Of course I am. All new parents go through a period of adjustment. Most of them get infants so they have to deal with colic and throw up, sleepless nights and feeding problems. With older children you have a whole different set of anxieties."

Riley pulled her around and settled her in his lap. The contact satisfied some of his intense need to touch her. It wasn't easy sleeping in the same room with a beautiful woman and keeping his hands to himself, but he was bearing up. "Yeah, like food fights and back talk and feeding problems."

"Some things they never outgrow," she teased. Her heart had started hammering the moment she dropped into his lap and she knew that if she didn't get out of the house soon, she wouldn't want to leave at all. She planted a brief kiss on his lips and jumped up. "I'll be late if I don't hurry."

Grabbing her lunch off the counter, she told him cheerfully, "Try not to have too much fun without me today."

"There's two chances of that happening."

"Only two?"

"Slim and none." She was almost out the door when he called, "Oh, Darcy! There's something I've been meaning to ask you."

"Yes?"

"Do other thirteen-year-old girls wear as much makeup as Jamaica wears?"

"Only if they're trying to get a job in a circus."

"That's what I figured."

The food fights slacked off, and the rest of the week was relatively uneventful for a war zone. Tyler and Jamaica settled in, Darcy adjusted to a new routine and Riley used humor to get them all over the rough spots. He tried to help out as much as his work allowed, but Darcy was still bone tired from working all day and trying to keep up the housework and the laundry at night. She was always in bed by ten o'clock and sound asleep by the time he joined her.

On Friday night, he stood beside her bed watching her sleep, caressing her in his thoughts, and wondering if things would ever settle down enough for him to put his plan into action. Arrangement notwithstanding, he clung to the hope that he could make Darcy's life at Cimarron so wonderful that she wouldn't dream of leaving. So far, he hadn't had much success in that department. She was gamely sticking by their agreement, but she seemed no closer to loving him, and that was scary.

She'd been marvelously patient with the children during the past few days, despite Jamaica's deliberate attempts to provoke her. The girl refused to take any interest in the ranch and sat around the house all day watching rock videos and grousing that there was nothing to do.

When he suggested that she might do some of the housework to help ease Darcy's burden, she'd retorted that if she'd known she was supposed to be an indentured servant she would have volunteered for the orphanage.

Tyler, on the other hand, seemed almost too eager to please. His clumsy attempts to help invariably resulted in even more work for the adults, but as Darcy told him, it was the thought that counted. He'd taken to making rounds with Riley and showed a bright curiosity about his surroundings and the workings of the ranch. Away from his sister's influence he was a lovable child—sweet, bright and hungry for affection.

But when the two were together, Tyler held back. He looked to Jamaica for cues as to how he should react. She responded by teasing and taunting and bringing out the worst in him. Darcy couldn't understand it, but Riley had a theory. Since Jamaica wouldn't allow herself to be loved, she didn't want Tyler to be on the receiving end of too much affection, either.

Aching with the need to talk to Darcy, to share his feelings with her, Riley sat on the edge of her bed and gently brushed a long lock of hair away from her face. He hoped she would wake up and he felt guilty for disturbing her. She stirred and sighed in her sleep and rolled onto her side.

"Darcy?" he whispered.

"Hmm?"

"I need you."

His words were as effective as a splash of cold water in her face. "Riley," she scolded as she rubbed her eyes.

"I don't mean I need your body. I do, but that's not what I want right now."

"What, then?"

"You. I'm lonely, Darce."

"How could anyone be lonely in this madhouse?"

"Can I hold you?"

She hesitated to invite him into her bed, knowing full well where such closeness could lead. "It's not a good idea."

"I just want to hold you tight and feel your heart beating close to mine. If it would make a difference, I'd settle for you holding me. I just need to know that I'm not alone in this."

Knowing she was asking for trouble, Darcy folded back the blanket and opened her arms to him. He snuggled down beside her in the narrow bed, sighed and rested his head on her breast.

She stroked his springy brown hair and smoothed her fingers over a cheek that was rough with whiskers. "You're not alone, Riley," she whispered in the darkness. "I'm here. Together we're stronger than we are separately. Together we can do anything. It's two against two, but we're bigger than they are."

"It hasn't been a very good week. Are you sorry you married me?" he asked tentatively.

She respected him too much to give a quick, pat answer. After a few moments she admitted, "Not sorry, but maybe worried about the responsibility."

"Me, too."

"Do you ever wonder if we're doing more damage than good where the children are concerned?"

"Sometimes. Then I remember my own childhood. Brody and I were even tougher little customers than Tyler and Jamaica when the Robertses took us in. But no matter what we did, no matter how terrible we were, they never gave up on us. They disciplined us and made rules and punished us when we broke them, but they didn't give up. The turning point for me came when I realized that their love wasn't conditional on my behavior. When I understood that it wouldn't be withheld no matter what, I no longer had to test it."

"Do you think that's what the children are doing?" she asked. "Testing us?"

"Maybe." He shared his observations about Tyler and Jamaica. "I think I could win the boy over if Jamaica would only allow it."

"Maybe we need to work on winning her over first."

"I was hoping you'd see things that way. I have an idea."

Darcy groaned. "Uh-oh."

"I was thinking that since tomorrow is Saturday, I'd spend the day with Tyler doing some male-bonding things, and you and Jamaica could do something together. Something that would show her you want to be her friend. What do you think?"

"I think it's good in theory but hard in application. Jamaica's made it pretty clear that she doesn't want to be my friend."

"Of course she does. She's just insecure."

"The little girl in *The Exorcist* was insecure." At his shocked look, she laughed. "I'm kidding, Riley. Actually it's not so bad. Mommies all over the world deal with this kind of stuff every day. I'll get used to it." She might even get used to Jamaica. Stranger things had happened.

He looked relieved. "All she needs is a little reinforcement to improve her self-esteem."

"Now you sound like Dr. Bradley."

"Well, we did pay him a lot of money for advice. We might as well use it."

"Okay. What do I have to do?"

"I'll leave that up to you. You know better than I what kind of activities appeal to girls her age." Riley nuzzled against her shoulder. "Gosh, I'm glad we got that settled."

Darcy groaned again. Settled? "What in the world am I going to do all day with a girl who's made it clear she'd rather eat worms than be in my company?"

"Shopping?" he suggested. "Girls like to shop, don't they?"

According to mall managers all over the world, they did. "I guess it's worth a try. There's one bit of parental wisdom the sage Dr. Bradley overlooked. If you can't win 'em, buy 'em."

He seemed to consider that for several moments. "Darcy?"

"Mmm?"

"I feel better already. Thanks."

She tightened her arms around him. Yes, he did feel good. Too good for comfort. "I think we'd better say good-night now," she hinted.

"Oh, sure. Good night." He made himself cozy and gave every indication of falling asleep.

"Riley! Get in your own bed now."

"Do I have to?" he asked wistfully.

"Yes." For both their sakes.

Two hours after their arrival at the mall, Darcy knew her mission was doomed. It had started when she'd gently suggested that Jamaica's makeup might be a bit much for a simple shopping trip. The girl became sul-

len and proceeded to make Darcy miserable. At the
shoe store she demanded a pair of pumps with stiletto
heels. She grudgingly settled for flats, but griped about
them for an hour afterward.

In every store they entered, the child insisted on
clothes that were far too old for her or were too outrageous for any age. She turned up her nose at Darcy's suggestions.

"I don't feel a black leather miniskirt is appropriate
for a seventh grader, Jamaica. The denim one is cute
and is much more acceptable."

"Yeah. To kindergartners and their grandmas."

The day was fast turning into a nerve-grinding con-
test of wills. Standing outside the dressing room in the
junior department, Darcy tried to remember what the
parenting book said about no-lose methods for resolv-
ing conflicts. After a lengthy dialogue in which she
used each of the recommended approaches without
success, she was ready to tear out her hair.

The rules were simply too hard to learn on the job,
she decided. And the job was too stressful. A person
needed years of intense training before attempting to
confront a teenager. Even a novice like Jamaica.

Jamaica finally stepped out of the dressing cubicle,
the disputed skirt in her hand. The sales clerk asked,
"Did you find anything you like, miss?"

"Yeah, this. Wrap it up." She thrust the skirt at the
clerk.

"I said you couldn't have that skirt," Darcy put in.

"I don't like the baby clothes you picked out for me,
so it's the leather or nothing."

"Very well." Darcy turned to the clerk. "Thank you for all your help. I'm sorry we won't be getting anything today, after all." She started for the door.

"Hey, wait a minute." Jamaica hurried after her. "Riley told you to buy me some clothes. I heard him. You can't just walk out."

"Yes, I can. I've been very patient with you, but since you seem determined to fight me every step of the way, I'm giving up. I'm willing to buy you whatever a girl your age needs, but that does not include black leather miniskirts and high heels."

"Where are we going now?" A note of worry had crept into Jamaica's voice.

"Home."

"Darcy, wait a minute."

Darcy stopped and turned. Tears slid down the girl's cheeks, leaving gummy tracks in the makeup that had earned her more than a few stares from passersby. All of a sudden, she didn't look like the defiant adolescent of every parent's nightmare. She looked like a frightened little girl, and Darcy's heart opened a crack.

"Yes?"

"How about giving me another chance?"

First, Darcy wanted an apology. She wanted to hear the words, "I am sorry," actually pass through Jamaica's lips. But she knew better than to press her luck. This grudging request was probably as close as she would get today. Jamaica was the child. She was the grown-up. She could afford to be generous. "Sure."

Things went a bit smoother after that, although Jamaica seemed to regret what she apparently considered a moment of weakness. When they passed a salon, the girl expressed a desire to get her hair styled. Looking at the girl's lank blond locks, Darcy decided a new haircut might be just what Jamaica needed to improve her self-image.

Darcy was prepared to explain the child's makeup to the stylist, but the woman didn't seem surprised or shocked by the excess.

"So what did you have in mind, sweetie?" the woman asked when Jamaica had been shampooed.

"That." She pointed to a picture on the wall of a hairstyle so short it would have looked extreme on a boot-camp inductee.

"Oh, no," Darcy cried in dismay.

"What's the matter with it?" Jamaica demanded, immediately defensive.

Before she could tell her it was just plain ugly, the stylist said, "That really wouldn't be a good style for your face shape." She fingered Jamaica's wet hair. "You have nice hair."

"I do?" The girl brightened.

"You sure do. What I suggest is a layered cut to add fullness around your face. You'd look like a movie star," she added as an inducement.

Jamaica appeared to consider. "Okay. Do it."

Darcy stood quietly by while the hairdresser snipped, feathered, moussed and blow-dried Jamaica's hair. The lady knew her business, and even little Miss Congeniality liked the results. The stylist handed Jamaica a mirror and swiveled the chair around so Darcy could get the full effect.

She was hesitant to say she liked it for fear her praise would rally Jamaica into another fight for the Marine Corps special.

"Well?" asked the stylist. "What do you think, Mom?"

Darcy's eyes met Jamaica's in the mirror, and the tentative smile on the child's face drooped into a frown. "She's not my mother. My mother's dead." With that she yanked off the styling cape and dashed out of the salon and into the mall.

Darcy gathered up their packages and quickly paid the bill. When she caught up with her, Jamaica was sitting on a bench, staring into a sparkling fountain. Darcy sat down beside her and said nothing.

After a while, the little girl whispered, "You're not my mother."

"No, I'm not."

"You're not even my stepmother since Riley isn't my real dad."

"You're right."

Jamaica turned to face her, and Darcy saw tears in her eyes again. "So what are you anyway?"

"I'm still trying to figure that out," she answered.

Jamaica sniffed. "You don't know dog-doo about kids."

"No, I don't."

"So why do you think you can be my boss?"

"I don't want to be your boss, Jamaica. Can't I be your parent?"

"No, thank you. Parents leave. My father left us when Ty was a baby. We don't even know where he is. Then Mom left us. I don't need any more parents."

"Do you need a friend?" Darcy asked softly as she placed her hand gently on the girl's shoulder.

Jamaica stared into Darcy's eyes for a long time as if doubting the sincerity of the offer. "I don't know," she said at last.

"I admire your honesty," Darcy told her. "If you decide you do need a friend, will you at least consider me?"

There was another long silence in which Darcy became aware of the other shoppers, the shrieking children, the bubbling fountain. When Jamaica's answer finally came, it renewed her hope for the future.

"Maybe."

Chapter Seven

Even though Riley's outing with Tyler was more successful than Darcy's with Jamaica, the events at the mall did initiate a tentative peace settlement between the two females. In the days that followed, overt acts of defiance were kept to a minimum and the girl grudgingly offered to help out around the house. They still weren't one big happy family, but it finally seemed possible that they might yet be able to learn to live under one roof.

The animals seemed to sense that they were there under sufferance and didn't cause too many problems. Darcy tolerated the noise and mess of Jamaica's parakeets on the condition that she assume responsibility for them. Beany proved devoted to Tyler. Darcy sometimes found herself tossing treats to the likable mutt and scratching his ears despite her resolve not to get involved with creatures of the canine persuasion.

When her notice at the bank was up, she said good-bye to her co-workers with mixed feelings. She would miss her friends, but she would definitely not miss the hassle of commuting. Her job as customer service representative had never been more than a way to make a living until she could devote all her energy to the thing she loved most. Music. Which she didn't seem any closer to doing. Maybe when the children started school she could spend more time at the piano. Hopefully the slower pace of country life would inspire creativity.

Now that she didn't have to hurry off to the bank each day, Darcy had more free time. More time to do the endless chores. More time to figure out how to keep the children entertained. But most of all, more time to be with Riley.

His wasn't a nine-to-five job, and he popped in and out of the house at all hours of the day and night with an unpredictability that unnerved her. He was always eager to help; in fact, he was worse than Beany when it came to following her around and waiting patiently for a crumb of attention. When she declined his assistance with some mundane chore, he was content to stand nearby and watch her, his warm brown eyes following her every move.

Invariably when she caught him gazing at her so intently, she was filled with the desire to invite him into her arms, smother him with kisses and see what developed. But since she never knew if he was lusting after her or admiring her housekeeping skills, she ignored her own desire and shooed him out of the house, claiming he was in her way.

Just to be on the safe side, she made a concerted effort not to be provocative. She stashed the silky nightgown in her bottom drawer and broke out her tackiest nightshirt. She twisted her hair into a knot on her head and wore patched jeans and Riley's old shirts while doing housework. Hoping Jamaica might take a hint, she limited her makeup to lip gloss and blush.

Her hausfrau guise didn't seem to lessen Riley's interest one bit. Not only that, but he was just as devastating as ever, and the more she was with him, the more she liked him. Oh, she'd loved him for a long time, but she hadn't really known him well enough to appreciate what a wonderful man he was. Now that he was free from the influence of alcohol, she discovered qualities his addiction had hidden—kindness, generosity, optimism and unfailing humor.

Loving was one thing, but liking and loving was a dangerous combination, and Darcy suffered daily from the tightly coiled need growing inside her. After three weeks as Riley's wife, things were still painfully unresolved between them. Tonight, as she climbed into bed, she was so frustrated that she wanted to pull the covers over her head and cry herself to sleep. But she couldn't cry silently, and Riley was sure to notice. Notice would lead to concern, and concern would lead to... well, where that would lead was what was so frustrating.

Riley strode into the bedroom, closed the door, leaned against it and sighed wearily. "What a day." He'd been at the barn all evening with a sick horse and when he'd come home, bone tired, the kids had started yammering at him.

It seemed Darcy had switched off the television and sent them to their rooms because they were fighting over the remote control. In the kids' dedicated couch-potato opinion, such punishment was cruel and unjust and they demanded instant relief. Understanding the importance of a united front, he had agreed with Darcy's stand. Tyler and Jamaica had returned to their rooms grumbling, and he'd gotten a headache.

"Some days it never lets up," he said as he tossed his hat on the dresser.

Although Riley had shown remarkable strength, Darcy realized that his need for alcohol could be renewed by too much stress. God only knew he'd had enough of that lately. "Sometimes I worry that I'm only adding to the problem with the children."

He shook his head and sank down on the side of his twin bed. "Nonsense. I'm just sorry that things are so rough for you."

"Don't worry about me, I'm pretty tough."

"Selfish beast that I am, I'm glad you're here for me, Darcy."

"I can't help but think you'd fare better with the kids without me. I thought we were making some progress, but after tonight I'm not so sure."

"Hey, it's been three weeks and their pictures aren't on milk cartons yet. I call that progress."

"I'm serious, Riley."

"So am I," he said sincerely. "I never would have made it without you to talk to, to keep me going."

"I want to help, but sometimes it seems like I'm just adding more burdens to your load."

"You're not still worried about your mother spending a few days with us, are you?"

She nodded.

"Well, don't be. I enjoy her company."

"A few weeks ago you were a carefree bachelor. Now you have a wife, two kids and a semi-invalid mother-in-law. That's a pretty big change."

He grinned through his fatigue, and that smile touched something deep within her. "Look at it this way. A few weeks ago I was all alone. Now I have a family."

She responded with a weak smile of her own. "You know, I don't remember you having such a gift for saying the right thing."

"There may be a lot of things you don't remember about me. We were apart for a while, darlin'."

Yes, too long. "I'm worried about what will happen with Mother here." When Ida's nurse had to go out of town for a few days, Riley had insisted the older woman stay with them at Cimarron.

"We'll all help you," he insisted.

"I'm not talking about taking care of her," she said softly.

He sat on her bed. Taking her hand in his, he asked softly, "Then what are you talking about?"

Maybe it was his tenderness. Or maybe the utter frustration of not being able to love him as she longed to. She couldn't say. But something caused her tear-filled eyes to overflow. "I just don't want her to worry about me when she goes home."

Despite his better judgment and knowing he would pay for his action with yet another cold shower, Riley pulled her into his arms and kissed her temple. "Don't cry," he pleaded huskily. Hoping levity might help, he added, "I promise not to beat you while she's here."

Darcy chuckled and turned her face into his neck. "See what I mean about always saying the right thing?"

Riley wanted to kiss her and keep on kissing her until she melted against him. He wanted to touch her, to caress her breasts and make wild love to her. Instead he held her away from him and looked into her eyes. "Tell me what's bothering you."

She didn't know how to answer. "She'll be with us for four days and nights. I'm afraid she'll suspect—"

"That we're not sleeping together?" he supplied.

"Yes. How can I explain that without telling her the whole truth?"

His grin was unarming. "That's easy to fix."

"We made a bargain, remember?" Constantly reminding herself, Darcy didn't think it would hurt to remind him, as well. Riley had been so supportive and helpful, so sweet and sexy, that her emotions were working overtime. The urge to tear him out of his clothes and have her way with him struck at the most unlikely moments. It was especially strong during likelier moments, such as this one when only inches separated them.

"I assure you, I haven't forgotten." The buildup of sexual awareness between them was driving Riley crazy despite Darcy's obvious attempts to downplay her beauty. That, she could never do. Even now as she sat cross-legged on her bed in a funny little-girl nightgown, she was the most seductive woman he'd ever known. "What do you suggest we do about it?"

"If I had an answer, I wouldn't be worried."

"As I see it, we have two choices. Since you're against consummating our marriage, the alternative is to put on a convincing act. So far we've been fairly successful.''

''Yes, but my mother is a more discerning audience than Tyler and Jamaica,'' she pointed out.

''Brody hasn't noticed anything amiss. Neither have Ruby and Dub or Glory and Ross. Everyone seems convinced that we're happy honeymooners.'' We're so good, Riley thought sadly, we even fool ourselves.

''Our acting ability might be good enough for an evening here, and afternoon there, a little hand-holding and a few pecks on the cheek. But, Riley, we're talking four whole days and nights.''

''I see what you mean.'' He ruffled a hand through his hair. ''Ida's going to expect more intimacy.''

''Exactly.''

''Well,'' he drawled, leaning closer, ''we'll just have to accommodate her.''

Darcy tipped up her head to see the devilment she knew would be in his eyes, but her gaze traveled no farther than the sensuous line of his mouth. He was so close she could feel his warm breath. A stillness overcame her as she waited for the kiss.

''I have an idea,'' he said in a husky tone. Plunging a hand into her hair, he tilted her head back. His gaze skimmed over her face, settled on her mouth.

''What are we doing?'' she whispered, afraid words might make him stop.

''Dress rehearsal,'' he murmured thickly.

Her lashes drifted downward. His lips found hers, gently rocking against them with loving force. The remembered sensations of Riley's kisses were never equal to the reality. The feel of his strong arms, the whisper of his breath, the taste of him, were even more delicious than she could ever conjure up in her mind. Her need was strong and she responded with a hunger that had gone unsatisfied too long.

Delightful shivers danced over her skin when his lips roamed her cheek to find the sensitive hollow below her ear. Darcy slid her hand into his sweat-dampened hair and pulled him to her. Turning, she searched for his mouth again, her lips trailing across his bristly cheek.

Riley ended her search by thrusting his tongue inside her mouth, but even that intimacy wasn't enough. It only made her hungry for more. Through his shirt, she felt the heat of his body, the solidness of his flesh. Intoxicated by his wild kisses, Darcy tugged apart the snaps on his shirt, right down to the waistband of his jeans. She felt the sharp intake of his breath when her hands slid onto the smooth skin of his chest.

He drew away slightly, and she no longer felt his roving hands on her back. She opened her eyes and realized her mistake when his bare shoulders came into view as he shrugged out of his shirt. She had let herself go, had forgotten that theirs was not destined to be a real marriage. But how could she stop now, when she wanted him so much?

The moment Riley touched the buttons on her gown, he felt her stiffen. He looked deeply into her eyes and saw her distress. He knew he could transform her uncertainty into passion, kiss her into submission. But he wouldn't do that. When they made love, he wanted to know that she was giving herself because she loved him, not because she was so carried away she couldn't help herself.

Riley cupped her face in his hands and kissed her gently, slowly. Then with all the willpower he possessed he pushed himself off her bed and stood. "I don't know about you, darlin', but I damn near forgot that was only a rehearsal."

Before she could comment, he turned toward the bathroom. At the door he paused and asked thoughtfully, "After that scene, are you still worried about our acting ability?"

She shook her head and smiled at him. "Riley?"

He didn't look at her for fear she might see the naked longing in his eyes. "Yeah?"

"Thank you," she whispered, marveling at his new perceptiveness, his gentleness, his amazing self-control.

"It was my pleasure," he answered softly, closing the door behind him.

And mine, she thought as she snuggled beneath the covers. With the love for him filling her heart and the taste of him still lingering on her lips, Darcy rolled over and pretended Riley held her in his arms while she slept.

Riley gave himself plenty of simmering down time before returning to the bedroom. He'd been thrilled by Darcy's response to his lovemaking, and her aggressive behavior when she'd unbuttoned his shirt told him that she was hurting as much as he was. A year ago it would have been enough, but now he wasn't satisfied to have her passion. He wanted her love and trust, as well, and he would wait.

Darcy's wish to pull off a successful charade for her mother's sake was just the chance he needed. For four whole days—and nights—he would be free to pull out all the stops. With a little time, a little patience and a lot of cold showers, he might just win her yet.

The following day when Riley came to the house for lunch, he caught Darcy with both hands full as she took a roasting pan from the oven. Taking every advantage of being her leading man in front of Ida and the children, who were busy setting the table, he cupped her face in his hands and kissed her at some length.

"Riley!" She tried to protest, but his lips were in the way. When she attempted to wriggle free, he held her fast.

He winked at her before backing off. "Thanks, I needed that."

"You're lucky I didn't burn you."

"But you did," he teased as he turned to face Ida and the kids. "Ty, do you see the steam coming out of my ears?"

"Yep," came the child's giggling agreement.

Jamaica busied herself with the napkins, trying her best to ignore everyone.

Ida beamed at her daughter and son-in-law. She was a sweet woman who spent most of her time in pain. On good days she had trouble doing the simplest tasks, but Riley had never heard her complain. "If you ask me, Darcy, I think the men in this family have been taking silly pills."

"I think you're right, Mom," she answered, fighting for the composure she always lost after one of Riley's unexpected caresses. "Maybe I should dose them with that disgusting tonic you used to give Cord and me. That would take the nonsense out of them."

"That disgusting tonic was a liquid vitamin-and-iron supplement," Ida declared defensively. "You and Cord were scrawny youngsters and had a lot of colds before I started that treatment.''

Glancing at an amused Tyler, Darcy said conspiratorially, "My brother and I would sneak into the kitchen and pour most of the vile stuff down the drain. But at the end of every bottle, just when we thought the torture was over, Mom produced another, just like a magician.''

Ida frowned. "I always wondered how we went through them so fast. If you weren't a grown woman, I'd paddle you for that.''

Riley obligingly smacked Darcy on the bottom. "You're never too old.''

"Riley!'' When she turned on him, he held up his hands and grinned. "Just thought I'd set an example for Tyler and Jamaica by showing them you're never too old or too big for a whomping.''

"That hurt,'' she lied, rubbing the offended area.

"Sorry, darlin'. Come sit down, I'll get the salad.''

He assisted Ida into her chair, then seated Darcy at the table with a flourish, the picture of the devoted husband.

After lunch Tyler and Jamaica surprised everyone by volunteering to clear the table. Darcy wasn't sure what prompted the gesture, but she was lavish with her appreciation. The children had taken to the gentle Ida at once and seemed eager to help the frail lady in any way they could. When they finished their task, they assisted her into the living room and talked her into telling them stories of her youth.

Riley helped Darcy load the dishwasher. "Have you noticed how protective the kids seem to be of your mother?''

"Yes, I have. This morning I shampooed Mom's hair and was in the process of blow-drying it when the phone rang. By the time I got back Jamaica was curling it with her own curling iron, and Tyler was supervising."

"That's a good sign, isn't it?" he asked. "If they can think about another person's needs for a change, doesn't it mean they're beginning to come out of their grief?"

"I'm no child psychologist, but it seems like a very good sign to me," she agreed.

Riley dropped the last plate into the dishwasher and put his arms around her waist. "Dare we assume they're finally accepting their new life?"

"I hope so." Darcy laughed nervously and pushed away to wipe the countertop. "I can finish up here. Don't you have something better to do?"

"Than hug you? Never. However, I do need to work on something in my office here at the house and I don't want to be disturbed. If you need me, just knock on the door. Don't come in."

It was out of character for Riley to be secretive. Usually he went out of his way to explain the workings of the ranch to her, at times even asking her untutored opinion. "All right."

"I thought you were going to help Noelle with the ranch accounts this afternoon. I heard Jamaica and Tyler say they'd entertain Ida for you."

Darcy glanced at the wall clock. "Gosh, I'd forgotten about that. I'll only be gone a couple of hours."

"You'd better hurry." Riley shooed her out the back door and waved goodbye, calling, "Take your time, darlin'."

Darcy enjoyed the hours she spent with Noelle and had no trouble grasping the ranch's bookkeeping system. But all during her sister-in-law's explanations, she found herself wondering what Riley was up to back at the house and why he wanted her out of the way.

"So how are things going on the home front?" Noelle leaned back and massaged her protruding abdomen.

"As well as can be expected." Darcy eyed her friend. "Are you all right?"

Noelle laughed. "Don't look so worried. The baby isn't due until the first of November, but the way she kicks and wiggles you'd think she was trying to rush things along."

Darcy smiled. Noelle already had two sons and always referred to her unborn child as she. "How can you be so sure it's a girl?"

"Because it has to be. Dusty and Danny have already put their order in for a little sister. Now, adept as you are at changing the subject, you don't get off that easily. How are things progressing between you and Riley?"

"They're not."

"Then kindly explain why Riley walks around with that dopey grin on his face all the time."

"Maybe he's happy he doesn't have to do his own laundry anymore?" Darcy suggested.

"According to Brody, Riley says he never dreamed he could be as happy as he is with you."

Darcy wished it were true, but she knew that he was just playing his role to the hilt for his brother's benefit. "Riley should have taken to the stage. It's all an act. One that will end in a few months."

Noelle shook her head. "I don't think so, Darce. He's always talking about the future and making plans."

"What kind of plans?"

"If he hasn't told you, I'm not going to let the cat out of the bag." Noelle struggled out of her chair and went to the little refrigerator in the corner. She got out a diet soda for Darcy and a carton of milk for herself. "How's Ida?"

Talk about changing the subject. Darcy wanted to pump her friend for more information, but she knew Noelle had said her last on the subject. "The new medicine she's taking seems to decrease the pain, but her mobility isn't much better. The specialist Riley brought in is talking about surgery after the first of the year, and the prognosis is good."

"I'm glad to hear it. That lady deserves the best."

"Tyler and Jamaica have been wonderful with her and have even been more communicative with me lately. Mom says I should just be patient. That they've had a rough row to hoe."

"Everyone they've ever loved has left them or let them down for one reason or another, " Noelle observed. "That has to be hard on children."

"That's what Dr. Bradley said during our last visit. He says they're looking forward to starting school, but they've yet to mention it to Riley or me."

"Give them time."

"I don't have that much time left," she said.

"Are you worried that they'll feel deserted again when you leave?"

Darcy laughed, but there wasn't much amusement in it. "Not really. I don't think they'll even notice when I leave. In fact, Jamaica will probably order out for pizza and celebrate.''

''Oh, come on, it can't be that bad.''

''I'm just afraid the stress will get to Riley.''

''He hasn't been drinking, has he?''

''Oh, no. But how much can a man be expected to endure?''

Noelle sipped her milk. ''I think you can stop worrying about his endurance. Riley loves you and I'm sure he intends to make things permanent.''

''I don't think so. He would have said something by now.''

''The Sawyer boys have a hard time revealing their deepest feelings. Don't forget, they had to overcome a childhood far more tragic than Tyler and Jamaica's.''

''I know.''

Noelle patted Darcy's shoulder. ''Stop torturing yourself, hon. Just love him and let him love you.''

''That would only make everything more difficult and you know it. I'll just have to bide my time.''

The next few days were like a miracle in the making. The interaction between her mother and the children never failed to amaze Darcy. Ida nurtured their poor bruised spirits with grandmotherly tenderness, and her frailty brought out the best in them. Eager to help and to please, they seemed almost content at last.

Every night, except for the evening Riley attended his AA meeting, he and the children locked themselves in his office to work on some secret project. Their happy laughter was like the music missing from Darcy's life, and she listened to it longingly, feeling excluded.

"What's the glum look for, honey?" Ida asked as Darcy joined her in the living room on the last night of her mother's visit. "Seems like you'd be happy Riley and the children are getting along so well."

"Oh, I am," she assured her mother too quickly. She'd spent another afternoon helping out Noelle, but when she was supposed to be working, she'd been thinking that they really didn't need her at all. A hired housekeeper could perform her tasks more efficiently, and her absence wouldn't even create a ripple.

"Whatever you say." Ida pretended interest in a magazine. "You're lucky, Darcy. Riley's a wonderful husband and father."

"Yes, he is," she agreed.

"And I've noticed a big change in Tyler's and Jamaica's attitudes just since I've been here."

"So have I," Darcy agreed.

"I should admit that I was a bit skeptical at first, but I see now that Riley has truly stopped drinking."

"Yes, I don't worry much about that anymore." Darcy felt guilty deceiving her mother about her and Riley's relationship and had to blink back tears. "Riley's a good man."

Before Ida could respond, the good man in question swept into the room and said, "Only good? That's a fine howdy-do." With that he produced a familiar black chiffon scarf and shook it out dramatically. "You know, Ida. These things are so big a person could make a whole outfit out of one if he needed to."

"They're big enough, but land, there's not much substance to them."

Riley laughed and Darcy blushed. He fashioned a blindfold and tied it around her eyes.

"What's going on here?" She giggled nervously as Riley guided her down the hall. The children snickered in their wake, and Beany frisked at their heels.

"Show a little patience, will you?" When Riley finally removed the blindfold it was with triumphant, "Surprise!"

Darcy blinked and the first thing she saw were the children's expectant, hopeful faces. The way her mother beamed, she knew Ida had been in on the whole thing. When she glanced at Riley he urged, "Well, how do you like it?"

She looked around the room. Riley's cluttered old desk had been replaced by a huge oak partners's desk with plenty of room for two. An electronic piano and bench stood against one wall, and in easy scooting range of the rolling desk chair was a personal computer, a printer, a large tape recorder and speakers. Every piece of equipment was festooned with big red bows.

Darcy was so surprised and bewildered she gasped. "What is this?"

Riley patted the console fondly. "This, my dear lady, is a computer processing system for composing and arranging music. The salesman said with this baby you'll be able to write or arrange anything from a simple song to a whole symphony. You can print out the text with the musical score or make your own demo tapes right in the system."

Darcy's hands crept up to her face. "I've heard of this, but I never dreamed of using one."

"Don't worry." Tyler quoted with a grin, "It's the most composer-friendly software available."

Darcy laughed and hugged the little boy close. To Riley she said, "So this is what you've been up to, redoing your office."

"It's not *my* office anymore, it's ours. Actually, I can't take all the credit. It was Jamaica's idea."

Darcy looked at the girl in surprise. "Yours?"

Jamaica ducked her head and looked embarrassed for the first time since her arrival. "Not really."

"Jamaica pointed out that you hadn't done much songwriting lately. She thought it was probably because you didn't have a quiet place to work," Riley put in.

"But this goes way beyond having a quiet place." Darcy's arm swept around the room.

Riley grinned. "Me and the kids put our heads together and decided we'd go into town and see what we could find that would make your job easier. You didn't really think all those trips were to pick up dog food, did you?"

"Are you surprised, Darcy?" Tyler wanted to know.

"I'm in shock," she confessed. "How'd you smuggle this stuff in here without me knowing about it?"

"I had it delivered this afternoon while you were with Noelle," Riley said. "The sales representative will come back at your convenience and teach you everything you need to know about it."

Darcy just shook her head in wonder.

"Don't you like it?" Jamaica asked shyly.

"I love it." With that she burst into tears. They'd done this for her. Not just Riley, but Tyler and Jamaica, too. All the time she'd felt left out of their fun and togetherness, they were plotting to surprise her with a gift so perfect it defied description.

Riley put his arms around her, and Ida began bustling the children out of the room. "What's the matter with Darcy, Ida?" Tyler asked. "Isn't she happy?"

"Oh, I think she's very happy," came Ida's soft reply.

Riley held her quietly. He had no idea what had gone wrong; his only thought had been to please her.

"I'm sorry, darlin'," he said when she finally looked up at him. "I didn't mean to make you cry."

"No, no, I'm the one who's sorry." She swiped the tears from her face with her hands. "I acted like such a baby."

"If you don't want to share the office, we can build on another room. I'd rather not convert the den because the kids and I thought it would be nice if Ida could stay with us more often."

"I'll be honored to share your office."

"I don't use it that much, and I promise not to distract you when you're working. You can change it around anyway you want."

Didn't he realize that just being in the same house with him was distracting? "I wouldn't change a thing, I love it just the way it is."

"Then what's wrong?"

"The expense. Equipment like this doesn't come cheap. You're too generous."

"Nothing's too good for my wife," he told her. "But you'll have to pay me back."

"How?"

"By writing some songs that'll make Nashville heads swim."

"That's a mighty tall order."

"Nothing you can't handle."

She flung her arms around him. "Oh, Riley, you're wonderful." And I love you, she almost added.

He smiled. "I must be getting better. Just a while ago I was only good."

Over a celebration cake the children had made during her absence, Darcy apologized for her outburst and explained how much she loved the office and the new music system.

Tyler smiled. "Ida already explained how you get weepy when you like something. She says that's why you write such beautiful songs. Will you play some for us?"

Darcy glanced at Jamaica, expecting her usual grimace. Instead the girl's eyes conveyed only warmth. "Not until she eats her cake."

Darcy's heart contracted to make room for blossoming hope.

Later the family gathered in the living room and Tyler fetched Darcy's guitar. She strummed a few chords and tuned up. "This song would sound better with a piano accompaniment, but I don't have enough hands for that."

"I can play if you want me to," Jamaica said hesitantly.

"You?" Riley, Darcy and Ida asked at the same time.

"Well, gosh, don't everybody look so shocked," she grumped. "I've been taking lessons for over two years."

"Why didn't you tell us you played?" Darcy asked her.

"I figured I wasn't as good as you, so what was the point?"

"If you want, I can arrange for you to take lessons again," Riley told her.

"I'd kind of like Darcy to teach me," she said softly. "That is, if it wouldn't be too much trouble."

Tears filled Darcy's eyes as she looked at the little girl who'd come so far in such a short time. "It wouldn't be any trouble at all."

Jamaica stopped on her way to the piano to give Darcy an impulsive hug, the first she'd ever offered. In many ways, it was the best present of all.

Riley sat quietly, enjoying the music and the strengthening family ties. At times like this, he forgot that it was all supposed to be temporary.

When he went into the bedroom, he could tell by the rapid rise and fall of her chest that Darcy was just pretending to be asleep. He had hoped the new office would convince her that he wanted her to stay. That she had a permanent place in his home as well as in his heart. He'd hoped she might let some of her defenses down in her excitement, but that hadn't happened. She obviously didn't want to talk to him. Or do anything else for that matter.

He crawled into his lonely bed and wondered how he could make things right between them. Sometimes he felt he was trying to spread himself too thin. Was winning the love of his wife and the trust of his children, while trying to help run a business, too much?

Somehow he had to succeed. His love for Darcy grew with each passing day, but a deal was a deal. He'd promised her that he wouldn't hold her to the wedding vows. That had been one of the conditions under which she'd accepted his offer in the first place. And he'd prove his trustworthiness by keeping their bargain. No matter how much it hurt.

Chapter Eight

Darcy spent a restless night staving off the nighttime demons whose taunts made her question her own actions. Good sense told her she was right to keep Riley out of her bed, but how could she satisfy the needs that held her in their hungry grip? Noelle had advised her to consummate her marriage, Riley had casually suggested the same thing and the rest of the world thought it was already a fait accompli. So what was holding her back?

Good sense again? Not exactly. In the hours before dawn, when it is hardest to be dishonest with oneself, Darcy admitted that the villain was her own fear. Fear that she loved Riley more than he loved her. Fear that the warmth and affection he'd shown her were more indicative of his acting ability than of his true feelings. Fear that if she didn't keep him out of her heart he

would break it again. She couldn't give in to loving him
when losing him would hurt so much.

But, the demons whispered, wouldn't never loving
him again be the biggest pain of all? And worse, what
if he continued to accept her refusal and gave up on her
altogether?

On their wedding night Riley had spoken of trust,
and that was an issue she had yet to resolve. Did she
dare trust him again? So far, his actions had proved
that his weakness for alcohol was a thing of the past.
His strict avoidance of the substance, coupled with his
faithful attendance of Alcoholics Anonymous meet-
ings, convinced her of his commitment. In every way
he'd shown how unlike her weaker-willed father he
really was and that his sobriety was something she
could believe in.

His dedication to his work was paying off, as well.
Not since he and Brody had founded Cimarron Training Stables more than ten years ago had the brothers
known such success. The quarter horses they trained
were winning races all over the country. Their dreams
of being the best in the business were close to being realized. Rebel's Redemption, the horse that had given
purpose to Riley's life, was now making him a wealthy
man. A golden future beckoned.

He'd also proven himself as a father. The selfish
young man he'd been only a year ago had turned himself inside out for the two children who needed him.
He'd gambled that patience and love would win out,
and tonight the payoff had come in like a glittering
Vegas jackpot. Even she, the outsider who had en-
croached the family circle, benefited from some of the

happy fallout. Jamaica and Tyler had finally scooted over to make room for her in their lives.

She should be blissfully happy. So why did she have a hollow place inside her? As soon as she asked the question, she knew the answer. She believed in everything but Riley's love for her. Actions were not enough. She had to hear him say that he wanted their sham marriage to be real. That he wanted her to stay with him forever. Was forever too much to ask for?

Before falling asleep, Darcy chided herself that she'd be better off channeling some of her angst into her music. She had no excuse not to work now that she had the perfect office, the perfect equipment, the perfect heartache. After all, her bizarre situation was the stuff hit country songs were made of.

When she finally entered the kitchen the next morning, Darcy found breakfast on the table.

"Good morning, sleepyhead." Riley set down mugs of coffee and kissed her cheek. For his mother-in-law's benefit, he lowered his voice to an intimate level and added, "You were sleeping so soundly, I didn't have the heart to wake you."

Ida smiled, and Darcy wondered what she'd think if she knew her daughter's fatigue was a result of sleepless soul-searching and not the activity Riley had hinted at.

"Sit down, dear," Ida said. "I believe Jamaica has everything ready."

Darcy glanced first at the food on the table and then to Jamaica who was trying hard not to look proud of herself. "You did all this?"

"Ida had to coach me." Jamaica accepted Darcy's hug of greeting with a self-conscious squeeze of her own.

Tyler slathered a fluffy biscuit with butter and took a big bite. "Hey, this isn't half-bad," he said with a full mouth.

"Coming from someone who eats mayonnaise on graham crackers that's not much praise." Jamaica's dry remark made the adults laugh, and it seemed to Darcy that she was surprised and pleased by their response.

"I may not be an expert on baking," Tyler said, "but I know what I like."

So did Darcy. She liked waking up to a noisy house full of people she loved. She liked the way good-natured teasing had finally replaced sibling violence. She liked starting her day with a kiss and a homemade biscuit.

She looked around the sunny kitchen, and the dark fears that came in the night seemed melodramatic and foolish. She belonged here, didn't she?

After breakfast Darcy watched the clock with mixed emotions. Ida's companion had offered to drive out to the ranch to fetch her and as the appointed hour approached, Darcy didn't know whether to feel relieved or sad that her mother's visit was over. She'd miss her, but once Ida was out of the house, Riley's attentions were sure to slack off to the nonexistent level. While she wouldn't miss the stress of knowing he was only pretending, she would miss the illusion of love he had created.

They said goodbye to Ida, and the children extracted a promise that she would come back soon. Riley and Darcy stood on the porch, watching the car drive away, and the children bounded off to their own pursuits. He suggested they have another cup of coffee before he went to work.

He poured, then sat at the table. Unaware that she watched him, he stirred sugar into his coffee, tasted it and added some more. His hands, slender and toughened by work, cradled the mug and Darcy knew that like the man himself, his hands could be both strong and gentle.

He never failed to take her breath away, even in moments as simple as this. She loved the crisp hair that still showed the mark of his comb. The soft dark cheeks scraped smooth by his razor. The warm brown eyes that seemed to look into her heart. Oh, Riley, she wanted to ask him, how can I leave in a few months when a lifetime of mornings like this wouldn't be enough?

When the phone rang, Riley answered. "Kids, it's your Aunt Marsha, and she wants to talk to you."

As oldest, Jamaica took the call and chatted with her aunt for several minutes. Then she said excitedly, "Hold on, I'll ask him." She covered the mouthpiece with her hand and turned to Riley.

"She wants to know if Tyler and I can go to Six Flags over Texas with her and the family."

"Yippee!" Tyler's feelings on the subject were clear.

"When?" Riley asked.

"They'll pick us up this afternoon and bring us back day after tomorrow." The look in her eyes told him how much she wanted to go. "Can we go? Please? That is, if Darcy doesn't mind taking care of the animals while we're gone."

Riley turned to Darcy, his uncertainty reflecting her own. "What do you think?"

She wasn't opposed to feeding the critters, but she thought it was crazy to send away the last of their chaperons just when they needed them most. But how could she say no to something as exciting as a visit to a giant amusement park? "School doesn't start until Tuesday, so I see no reason why they shouldn't go."

Arrangements were made, and the children launched themselves into Riley's and Darcy's arms with grateful hugs before hurrying to their rooms on a mission of frantic packing. Within a few hours they were gone, trundling away in the Leggett family van, headed for Dallas, Texas, and a last fling before school started.

After straightening up the suddenly quiet house, Darcy thought she might spend some time at the keyboard. All her misery of the night before had given her an idea for a song. But she didn't want to shut herself in the office until she was sure of Riley's plans.

She felt guilty about his missing the All-American Futurity in Ruidoso, New Mexico, this year, but he had insisted that Brody could handle it alone. The brothers had worked out a plan whereby Brody would assume most of the responsibility for running Cimarron until school started. Then Riley would take over to give Brody more time to be with Noelle before and after the baby came.

Darcy knew he was sacrificing New Mexico because he didn't want to leave her alone with the children, but now that they were gone he had no real reason to stay.

"Why don't you catch a late flight to New Mexico?" she suggested as they made sandwiches for lunch.

"Why would I want to do that?" he asked in surprise.

"Well, it is the most important race of the year."

"Are you trying to get rid of me?" he wanted to know.

They stood side by side at the counter, and he slathered mayonnaise on bread while she sliced tomatoes and tore off lettuce leaves. When the sandwiches were ready she carried the plates to the table.

"No, but it seems unnecessary for you to hang around here now with the kids gone." She ate her sandwich and avoided his eyes.

"You're still here," he pointed out.

"You don't have to stay on my account."

"Maybe I want to stay. Maybe I can't think of any place I'd rather be than here with you."

"You can ease up on the mushy stuff, Riley, we don't have an audience anymore."

"That's the main reason I don't want to go to Ruidoso." Riley knew what she was saying made sense, but Brody didn't really need him, and leaving Darcy now seemed suddenly unthinkable. "We need to talk, Darcy."

"About what?"

"About our situation. I've been doing a lot of thinking and I believe a few changes might be in order. We've been married less than a month and I already regret that proposal."

She looked away from him. These were not the words she'd wanted to hear. "I see."

Riley immediately realized that she had misunderstood and hastened to clarify. "I don't mean I'm sorry

I married you, darlin'. But I do regret making it a marriage of convenience."

"What are you trying to say, Riley?" Not daring even so much as a glimpse at him, she pretended interest in her lunch.

"I think we're both adult enough to admit we haven't lost the physical attraction we've always shared."

So he was aware of the daily battles between her good sense and her libido? It must be gratifying for him to know she was much weaker than he in that department. She tried to eat, but found she'd lost her appetite.

When she didn't comment, Riley continued. "If anything, the attraction is stronger than ever, so why are we beating ourselves silly trying to deny it?"

"You tell me."

"We need each other, Darcy. At least, I need you." He wanted to tell her how much he loved her, but considering that cornered-doe look in her eyes, he was afraid those words might send her out of the house and out of his life. Since he'd beat the booze, he'd felt on top of the world, like he could do anything. His work, the kids, all made his life full and good. He'd only failed at one thing.

He hadn't made Darcy love him.

She thought about his words. He needed her; it was as simple as that. Being an honorable man, Riley wouldn't dream of seeing another woman now that he was married. And didn't she have needs, too? Didn't she lie awake each night, aching with the need to touch him, to love him?

"Why shouldn't we express our feelings if we both have them?" he asked. Then softer, he said, "I know you still do."

At that moment Darcy almost wished Riley weren't so damned honorable. How much easier it would be for her to break that promise to herself, if he would only throw in the word love. Even if he didn't mean it.

"I don't want to talk about this anymore." She felt dangerously close to tears, so she jumped up and skidded her plate onto the counter before running out of the kitchen. Riley caught up with her as she ducked into their shared office.

"Don't be mad at me, Darce."

"I'm not mad at you, Riley."

"I just want to be your husband. In every sense of the word. Is that wrong?"

"It's not wrong, but it does seem cold-blooded." She stared at the slim brown hands holding hers.

With his forefinger, he lifted her chin until their eyes met. "I promise you that the blood coursing through my veins is hotter than a fifty-dollar diamond. Do you want me as much as I want you?"

Want. Need. Never love. Darcy couldn't speak, she could only nod and hate her weakness. His lips lowered to hers, and she felt his tongue gently trace the soft fullness of her mouth. The tension went out of her and she became as warm and drowsy as a cat on a sunny windowsill. While she could still reason, she asked herself where it was written that love had to be equal. The way she felt about Riley, maybe hers would be enough.

Through the soft fabric of her blouse Riley's fingertips circled around her breast, and he felt it surge as though eager for his touch. He deepened the kiss and felt her tremble against him. His hands in her hair drew her head back to expose the hollow at the base of her throat and he kissed her there before parting her blouse to brush his lips along her shoulder.

Fighting for control, he tried to remind himself that this wasn't the way it was supposed to happen. He'd promised himself not to take advantage of her desire and here he was, doing just that. They were married, and he loved her. They belonged to each other. This was right.

Riley slipped one hand beneath her shirt to unfasten the front clasp of her bra and released small breasts that were swollen and firm and welcoming. After only a moment of uncertainty, he accepted their invitation by picking her up and carrying her into their bedroom.

As her feet touched the floor, his hands swept down the sides of her body, then roamed over her hips and her tiny waist. "It's good between us." His voice was a ragged version of his desire. He held her gaze with his as he massaged her breasts through her blouse with infinite slowness. "It was always good between us."

He turned away from her long enough to shove the twin beds together. Only with Darcy had he ever felt this kind of passion. Passion that stripped away all remnants of reason. When he'd finished his task, he stood tall before her. "Do you want this, Darcy?"

She hesitated, trembling, aching, needing. "I want you," she whispered.

His steady gaze told her that she would have to make the next move. Tentatively she reached out and slowly unbuttoned his shirt. She slid it off his arms and dropped it to the floor. Her blouse followed and in time, the rest of their clothing.

The sense of homecoming Riley felt as he stretched out beside her on the bed was almost a physical ache. He lowered his head and watched as her eyes fluttered closed, as her lips parted in anticipation. Gently he kissed her temple, then the curve of her eyebrow. Without haste he explored her face, enjoying the feel of her soft skin beneath his lips.

She gasped when their lips finally met, and with a moan, Darcy slipped her hands into his hair, seeking more pressure. She arched against him as his fingers trailed along her thigh, and familiar ribbons of desire vibrated along every tautly stretched nerve.

Passion engulfed her as his mouth crushed down on hers. The pace he set was languorous, enervating. It was meant to prolong their pleasure and give them time to savor the joy they shared. He kissed her breasts and too soon left them moist and aching as his lips fanned across her collarbone, to first one shoulder and then the other.

Her whole body sung with a desire so primitive that it tore through her with the power to obliterate all thoughts but one. Pleasure. Seeking it, demanding it, Darcy moved beneath him, her hands exploring his well-muscled body.

Their passions equal, their need the same, they finally became one again as they were always meant to be. Bodies burned and tensed. Breathy sighs became moans, then whispered names. They were desperate to touch and be touched and they moved slowly, allowing the fire to build to the flashpoint.

Darcy's driving need for fulfillment matched Riley's, and in the moments before they found it she experienced an overwhelming joy. The doubts and fears of the past could never diminish her love for him.

Giving themselves up to the release, they clung together for several long moments. As Riley regained the use of his mind, he wondered at the powerful experience they had just shared. Darcy had given herself to him completely, without restraints. How he loved the sweet woman in his arms. He had to tell her, to make her understand that without her nothing else mattered.

"Darcy, I love you," he whispered against her hair. He waited for her answer, but it didn't come. Worried that she didn't share his feelings, he leaned over her only to find she had drifted gently into a lover's sleep. Maybe it was just as well that she hadn't heard his heartfelt declaration. She was distrustful of words. And everyone knew, actions spoke the loudest.

An hour or so later, Riley woke up first, feeling rested and complete. Afternoon sunlight slanted through the window and bathed the bed in gold. "We *are* good together," he murmured. "Even after all this time."

"Yes," she agreed drowsily without moving.

"Do you still think I'm cold-blooded?" He tightened his arms around her and squirmed against her.

"Riley!"

He kissed her neck noisily. "Do you?"

"What if I said yes?" she asked, laughing.

"Then I would just have to prove to you how hot-blooded I really can be. What's your answer?"

"Yes!"

Riley was honor bound to prove himself. After a quick phone call to Billy Sixkiller he took the rest of the afternoon to do just that.

Their lovemaking was beautifully intense, but that night Riley couldn't help wondering if anything had really changed. Physically they were as intimate as two people could be, but emotionally he yearned for more. He wanted commitment, but Darcy's manner indicated that she wasn't comfortable with their new intimacy and he didn't know why.

While Darcy gave free rein to her sensations, basking in the sensual world Riley had shown her, she knew she had to hold back her emotions. She succeeded by reminding herself that as far as he was concerned, they had merely been exercising their marital rights.

This afternoon had been a taste of heaven, but this uncertainty was pure hell.

When Riley returned to the bedroom after his shower that night, he noticed that Darcy had pushed the beds apart again. Before he could question her, she said, "You know, I've been thinking. Maybe you should go on to Ruidoso. I know Brody would like to have you with him as much as you'd like to be there."

He toweled his head. "Darcy, we went through this earlier."

"I know, but with the kids gone there's no reason for you to be here." She tried to inject a note of flippancy in her tone. "Besides, I need the time to work. My agent's been bugging me to send him some more songs, but what with all that's been going on around here, I haven't had a chance to write. It would be such a relief to have the house all to myself."

But it would be wretched to be alone, to sleep alone. She had to let him know that she wasn't going to get all clingy and possessive because of a little ecstasy.

Her words hurt Riley, but he managed to hide it. He felt guilty about the fact that she hadn't been working and knew he was largely responsible. Him and the kids. Of course she wanted to be alone. Hadn't she made it clear that she was only here to hold up her end of the bargain? He'd been a fool to let the abandon with which she'd made love to him lull him into a false sense of security.

"What about the kids' school?" he asked.

"They're already enrolled and they have their supplies. All I have to do is pack their lunches and see that they get on the right bus."

"I don't know."

"Of course, if you think I can't handle it—"

"It's not that." He didn't doubt her competence. He doubted her motives. Obviously today hadn't meant as much to her as it had meant to him.

"Do you think the kids will understand?" he asked.

"I'll explain. Don't worry, you'll be home midweek."

"All right, if that's what you want, Darcy. Tell them we'll take a trip next weekend."

"What kind of trip?" she asked suspiciously.

"I've been telling them how much fun Brody and I used to have at Roman Nose State Park when the Robertses took us there. They've asked to go, but so far it hasn't worked out. We'll go over the weekend. That is, if you have no objections."

His tone of voice irritated her, and she slipped into bed and turned her back to him. "I have no objections," she muttered.

Riley flung himself into bed and snatched at the covers so hard they came untucked and his feet protruded. Mumbling, he got up and remade the bed, wondering all the while what he had done wrong. He looked at Darcy and thought he saw her shoulders heaving. Was she crying? God, he would never understand the woman.

Softening his tone, he whispered, "Good night, Darcy."

"Good night, Riley," came her even softer reply.

Chapter Nine

Riley managed to get an early flight to New Mexico the next morning. He declined Darcy's offer of breakfast as well as her help with packing, claiming he'd done it so many times he knew exactly what he needed. His clipped responses to her verbal overtures let her know he was in no mood for small talk.

She watched him pack, feeling dejected and wanting so much to touch him, to do anything to relieve the tension between them. She couldn't bear to see him leave with things so unsettled. "Why are you so angry?"

"I'm not angry." Zipping his flight bag with more force than necessary, he yanked it off the bed and faced her. He had lain awake last night long after Darcy was sleeping soundly. Their lovemaking had seemed so right that he'd fooled himself into thinking things were going to work out. But when he'd seen the beds pushed apart, when he'd heard her urging him to go, he knew how wrong he was.

"Then you're a better actor than I thought," she commented dryly.

He stared at her, and a muscle clenched in his jaw. Darcy noticed that he clutched the handle of the bag so tightly that his knuckles showed white through his tan. Her heart pounded, and her mouth went dry. The air in the room suddenly seemed electrified, and waiting for him to speak was like waiting for the crash of thunder.

"I'll tell you what I am, Darcy," he said at last. "In a word, I'm confused. I don't like being confused. For some reason I got it into my head that last night might have meant something to you."

Even as he spoke, a cautious internal voice warned Riley not to force her hand. If he pushed for a confrontation and got it, he might not like the results.

"Last night was special." Darcy looked away. His eyes held a new bitterness that she couldn't deal with. Despite the intimacies they'd shared, he was still a puzzle to her, one she feared she'd never understand. Yesterday he'd been so gentle and loving, but this morning he'd slipped into his tough-guy mode as easily as he had slipped into his worn denim jacket.

"Then what the hell is this all about?" he demanded. His harsh words almost made him miss the quiet inner voice warning him to slow down. He'd learned in AA how important it was to talk about problems. He didn't think he could talk rationally about this one.

He zeroed back in on Darcy just as she said, "I'm confused, too, okay? I need time to sort things out and to figure how last night fits into the agreement we made.''

"Oh, now I get it." The damned agreement again. He knew he didn't want to talk about that. Or about Darcy's regrets. He grabbed his other bag and headed for the door. He didn't have to stand here and listen to her weigh the pros and cons of loving him.

"Riley?" Darcy called after him. "Why are you leaving like this?"

"I'm giving you what you want. I'm going to New Mexico so you can have the whole house to yourself, just like you want. I'm giving you the time and the space you want. So be my guest and think about things to your heart's content."

She hardened her voice. "Don't, Riley."

He stood at the open door, torn between going and staying. Between what felt right and what was right. He dropped the bags to the floor and pulled her into his arms. He held her face firmly in his hands and kissed her with all the pent-up frustration he felt.

"And while you're at it, think about that."

The sensuous kiss was over too soon, and before Darcy had quite recovered, Riley was gone.

The hours ticked by slowly. Darcy wandered through the house, but it was too full of reminders of Riley for her to find any peace. Finally she decided to make the best of a bad bargain, and feeling sick at heart she secluded herself in the office. Hoping left-brain activity would force her errant thoughts away from him, she opened the user's guide that had come with the new computer equipment.

She read and studied the book until all the jargon made sense. She'd used a computer at the bank and was not a complete novice. She'd need an expert to help fine-tune her operating skills, but after several hours she was confident enough to boot up the system and try her hand at the music keyboard. In a short time, she was amazed at what she could do with the synthesizer and loved the freedom it gave her to arrange and simulate other instruments.

She soon developed a creative momentum that lifted her spirits and took her far away from her problems. As she slipped out of depression, ideas began to flow.

She'd talked to other musicians about the creative process. Some started with music, others with words. But Darcy almost always conceived them as one, the song evolving as the words in her heart found structure in the music in her mind. The computer program seemed to speak the language of music, which facilitated the translation of that mental song into notes on paper. By the time hunger drove her from her work early that evening, she had written one piece that she thought was pretty good.

She took a sandwich and glass of milk back to the office and played the tape of the music over and over as she ate. Then she made another tape on which she also sang the lyrics.

When she listened to that, she recognized problems with phrasing and timing and heard inconsistencies of meter, which she quickly corrected. When she replayed it yet again, she experienced a powerful feeling that told her "Heart on the Line" was better than pretty good. It could be a hit for the right singer.

She immediately thought of K. C. Maguire, the star who was unknowingly responsible for Darcy returning to Oklahoma and to Riley.

Riley. She hadn't been so absorbed in her work that she hadn't thought of him constantly throughout the day. In truth, he had been her inspiration. Memories of his loving and the way he made her feel had put emotion into the poignant lyrics. The pain she'd felt when he left became the haunting music.

Riley.

She didn't have long to dwell on her problems. The children returned on Sunday evening full of excitement. Darcy suspected that Marsha had extended the invitation to Six Flags to assuage some of her guilt at having given them up. If that were true, neither Jamaica nor Tyler seemed to notice. They both talked at once about the wonderful things they'd done.

When they finally paused for breath, Darcy said, "So I take it you two had a good time."

"It was great." Tyler gushed some more about his favorite ride, the Texas Cliff-hanger. Then he said quietly, "You know, Aunt Marsha is nice and stuff, but I'm glad I'm home."

"Me, too," Jamaica put in. "The cousins fight all the time. I don't know how Aunt Marsha and Uncle Bill stand them. Joey is such a brat, and Molly is so picky she won't touch anything that isn't drowned in catsup."

"Kevin and Jill call each other names that even I never heard of," Tyler said earnestly.

"Being in a van with them is like being in a cage with a bunch of monkeys." Jamaica's tone said she was beyond such antics.

Darcy just smiled.

"It's good to be home with normal people." Tyler's emphasis on the word normal made Darcy smile again.

The children had no trouble accepting Riley's absence. They remembered how important the All-American Futurity was to Cimarron. When he called just before bedtime, they had to relate the highlights of their trip all over again. Finally Jamaica handed Darcy the phone.

"He wants to talk to you," she said before urging Tyler off to bed.

Darcy held the receiver for a long moment as she tried to compose her thoughts. Total absorption in her music had purged her of much of the pain of her uncertainties. Composing always took her out of herself and helped to put things in perspective. When she answered, the first thing out of Riley's mouth was, "I miss you."

"I miss you, too," she answered honestly.

"I never should have left with things like that between us and I want to say I'm sorry." He wanted a lot more than that, but he'd settle for her accepting his apology.

"What happened wasn't your fault."

"It doesn't matter if it was or not. I'm sorry and I miss you like hell."

Or did he miss sharing her bed? As soon as the thought leaped unbidden into her mind, Darcy pushed it out. She latched on to a neutral subject. "Good luck tomorrow. The kids and I are going over to Noelle's to watch the race on the sports network. We'll be looking for you and Brody in the winner's circle.''

"We might just be there. He's pretty sure we can make this win four years in a row.''

"Brody's a smart guy,'' she said softly.

"Look, Darce. We need to talk when I get back. We have things to work out.''

"We do at that.''

She sounded breathless, and Riley wondered what she was thinking. But he didn't dare ask. He'd learned his lesson. "I'll be home Friday. Will you think about me while I'm gone?''

"You're the only thing I can think of.''

The All-American Futurity, billed as the million-dollar horse race, was run the next day at Ruidoso Downs. High Dollar Man, trained at Cimarron Training Stables, crossed the finish line first. Random Violence, also trained at Cimarron, crossed second, which gave the Sawyer brothers their first one-two finish.

Riley and Brody were so thrilled by what the win would mean to Cimarron that they hardly had time to think about their ten percent share of the purse or the fact that their future financial security was now assured.

Darcy hurried the children home after the broadcast in hopes that Riley would call. She wasn't disappointed. He was pumped up and full of excitement. They talked so long—and so longingly—that the recent friction between them seemed irrelevant. When she accused him of trying to spend the whole purse on one phone call, he claimed it was the next best thing to being there and then made her blush with his promises of how they would celebrate his victory when he got home.

Riley hung up the phone and flopped back on the motel bed. He'd made only a brief appearance at the owner's wild party down the hall. Last year he would have been the last to leave, and the first to call for another round of celebration drinks.

Tonight, intoxicated by life and its endless possibilities, he'd happily turned down everything from champagne to beer. When he'd finally had all the congratulations and backslapping he could take, he'd left Brody to bask in the glory.

Slipping away unnoticed, he had raced to the phone. After hearing Darcy's voice, he knew he had reached the milestone the counselor at the clinic had promised him. In a way, the victory was as great as winning the Futurity.

He no longer need alcohol. Plain and simple.

On Friday, Jamaica wandered into the kitchen where Darcy was putting the finishing touches on a chocolate cake for Riley's homecoming.

"I've got a problem, Darcy."

She swirled the frosting with a knife to cover the wave of gladness she felt that the girl had turned to her for advice. "What is it?"

Jamaica bit her lip. "The kids at school aren't very friendly to me."

"You've been there less than a week. Give them time."

"I don't think forever will be long enough."

Darcy knew that feeling well. "It's a rural school district. Maybe the kids feel a little intimidated by the fact you come from a big-city school."

"I don't think that's it." Jamaica shoved her hands into the back pockets of her jeans. "The guys are friendly enough, but the girls snub me."

"I see." She had hoped Jamaica's use of makeup would taper off as she adjusted to her new life, and it had. And then school started and she'd gone back to her old excesses. In a moment of insight Darcy had finally understood that until Jamaica was completely sure of herself and her appearance, the girl would continue to hide behind a cosmetic mask. Darcy chose her next words carefully.

"Do the other girls wear makeup?"

"You aren't going to start in on that again, are you?" Jamaica's tone was petulant, and Darcy feared she would turn away. She couldn't let that happen.

"I just wondered, is all."

"How I look is my business, no one else's."

"I won't presume to tell you what to do about anything as personal as makeup. I just want to help you with this problem. Maybe the girls think you're too sophisticated for them."

"Maybe."

"Or it could be they're jealous."

"Then that's their problem," she said with a defiant look.

"You have a point there." Darcy patted the girl on the shoulder. "Will you set the table while I add vegetables to the roast in the oven?"

Jamaica took down plates. "I'm not going to start looking like a frump just because a bunch of country bumpkins are jealous."

"Good for you." Darcy tested the meat, added the peeled vegetables and slid the roasting pan back into the oven. "You don't want to look like one of the crowd, you want to stand out. Be different."

Jamaica fell silent as she laid out the silverware. Darcy hoped she was also digesting that last observation.

"Their mothers probably won't let them wear makeup."

"Probably not."

"That's mean. A girl should be able to do what she wants."

"I'm nobody's mother," Darcy reminded her, "but I can see the mothers' position. They hate to see their children grow up too soon. Adult responsibilities come fast enough without rushing into them."

When Jamaica failed to comment, Darcy was encouraged to go on. "Parents need to feel that they can protect their children from the bad things in life. When they see them growing up and looking and acting like adults, they have to acknowledge that they will lose them someday. That makes all parents, but especially, mothers sad."

"Are you saying the girls at school don't wear makeup because their mothers love them?" Jamaica had drawn the right conclusion, but she seemed baffled by it and a little contemptuous.

Darcy smiled and shrugged. "Having never had a child of my own, I can't say for sure. It's just a theory I have."

Jamaica continued to set the table, but in a few minutes she looked amazed, as if possessed of a wonderful revelation. "You and Riley are always giving me a hard time about my makeup." It was a statement of the obvious.

"Riley and I care about you," Darcy said simply.

"Yeah." Jamaica nodded and a wide smile transformed her features for a moment before they dissolved in a frown. "But you still haven't told me how I'm going to make the girls at school like me."

"You can't make someone like you, honey." You can't make someone love you, either. "But I have an idea. Maybe between the two of us we can come up with a compromise that's acceptable to you and the girls at school."

Jamaica followed Darcy into her room and took a seat at the dressing table. "What if I don't like your idea?"

"Then you can ignore it." First Darcy taught her the correct way to remove the heavy cosmetics. She'd been itching to do this for weeks. Jamaica was too pretty a girl to hide behind a mask. That task was accomplished with a short lecture on the importance of skin care.

Jamaica surveyed her naked face in the mirror. "Now I look as dowdy as the rest of them." The words were voiced as a complaint, but Darcy suspected Jamaica was relieved to have a chance to fit in with her crowd. Especially if she didn't have to take responsibility for the change.

"Wait until we're finished." Darcy pulled a little blue cosmetic bag out of her bottom drawer, unzipped it and dumped the contents on the dressing table.

"This is all new stuff," Jamaica observed.

"Yes, I bought it for you."

"For me? When?"

"The week after you arrived."

While Jamaica thought about that, Darcy brushed rose pink blush on her fair cheeks and deftly applied a slick lip gloss. Then she brushed the tips of her long lashes with the mascara wand.

"Well, what do you think?"

Jamaica turned this way and that, scrutinizing herself critically in the mirror. "I'm pretty," she gasped.

"Yes, you are."

Jamaica blinked away the tears that would spoil her new look. "I looked stupid before, didn't I?"

"Not stupid. Never that."

"Why didn't you tell me I was wrong?" she wanted to know.

"I didn't think you were ready to listen."

"Oh, Darcy!"

When Darcy opened her arms, Jamaica propelled herself into them with an injured child's need for security. Darcy welcomed her with a loving mother's tenderness.

Riley had slipped into the house unannounced with the thought of surprising his family. It was he who was surprised. He stood quietly, observing the scene between Darcy and Jamaica, and wanted nothing more than to be included in the circle. But he knew this private moment was an important one and so was able to resist the temptation to intrude.

After a few moments he stepped down the hall and reentered with a noisy, "Hey, is anybody home?"

"Riley!" Jamaica ran to hug him.

He held her at arm's length and pretended to get a load of her face for the first time. "You look great, punkin. Now I can see your natural beauty shining through."

"Do you really like it?" she asked shyly, obviously needing his approval.

"Yes, I do," he said around the lump in his throat. When he glanced at Darcy he noticed a suspicious gleam in her eyes.

"I'll go tell Tyler you're home." Jamaica raced out of the room.

With a hopeful shrug, Riley held out his arms toward Darcy. "Come here and pretend you're glad to see me."

"I don't have to pretend," she said against his mouth as he lowered his head to kiss her. A kiss that ended abruptly when Tyler burst into the room.

"I'm glad you're home, Riley, we missed you."

Riley put an arm around him and hugged the boy to his side. "All of you?"

Darcy met his gaze and saw the yearning in his eyes. "Every one," she confirmed.

Riley told them all about the races over the special dinner. This time no one even suggested switching on the television, and Darcy experienced some of what her own mother must have felt during meals shared with her husband and children.

So this was what it was like to create a family, she thought. Maybe she and Riley had gone about it all wrong, maybe they'd done it backward and clumsily, but the results had been worth it. In a few months, when she had to leave, she could do so with the knowledge that she had helped this family find one another. It wouldn't take away the pain, but it would help her through the lonely days.

In response to Riley's inquiry about how she had spent her week, Darcy played her new song for him and the kids. She didn't mention that she'd already sent a tape to her agent in Nashville. It could make the rounds for months before she heard anything and she didn't want to get their hopes up.

Riley was quiet when she finished. "Well?" she demanded. "How do you like it?"

He looked at her with new insight. That music, those words, had come from her heart. Only someone in love could have written that song. "It's beautiful."

"Is that all you have to say?" she teased.

"It's got hit written all over it," he ventured.

"Superhit," Tyler chimed in.

"Megahit," piped up Jamaica.

"Well," Darcy said with mock offense. "That's more like it."

Riley stretched his arms over his hand and yawned. "I think we should make a night of it."

"Gee, it's only nine o'clock," Tyler complained.

"It's not even a school night," Jamaica pointed out.

"That's true, but we're leaving early in the morning for Roman Nose Park, or did you forget?"

"We didn't forget," Tyler told him. "Darcy helped us pack our stuff today."

"Good. So now you don't have anything left to do but get a good night's sleep. Besides, I've had a long week." With a meaningful glance at Darcy, he added, "I can't wait to sleep in my own bed again." With that he shooed the children to their rooms and led Darcy to the one they shared.

He opened the door and whisked her inside. Before she had a chance to demand the talk he'd promised, he took her in his arms. The fiery intent of his kisses told her how painful their separation had been for him. She matched him kiss for kiss with a hunger that made her want to forget there were any problems in the world. When he drew away, her lips were moist and heated.

"It's still good," he murmured against her neck.

"Always." She whispered the word in hopes that whoever was now in charge of her fate would hear and make it come true. God, how she wanted always. She tipped back her head, giving Riley full access to her neck. He smelled so good, felt so wonderful, and she was again transported into a realm of delicious sensations.

Riley ignored his own advice about getting a good night's sleep and it was hours later before they finally did so. Drained by passion and refilled with amazing completeness, they finally slept, wrapped in each other's arms and the warmth of their loving.

Chapter Ten

They left for Roman Nose Park right after breakfast the next morning. Since Riley's pickup truck didn't have a back seat, they opted to take Darcy's little car, quickly filling the trunk and the luggage rack with a lot of stuff they probably wouldn't need on an overnight trip. It was an unseasonably crisp day, a golden taste of autumn tacked on to the tag end of summer.

They traveled northwest to El Reno and then northwest again to Watonga. Everyone was in high spirits, but Riley soon discovered that while his objective had been family togetherness, a long car trip in which four people were confined in the limited space of a subcompact was not the best way to achieve it.

Just outside Watonga, another squabble broke out. Tyler and Jamaica couldn't agree on which radio station to listen to. Tyler wanted a country-western station in the hope of hearing Darcy's song, "Love and Other Long Shots," and Jamaica wanted rock.

Majority ruled, and an all-country station was tuned in. After twenty minutes or so, Jamaica got restless and began making fun of the lyrics of the songs.

"Why is every country song about somebody's misery?" she wanted to know.

"Because love is a very powerful emotion," Darcy explained. "Country songs express it in a way people can understand. It's the poetry of the heartland."

"The words are so dopey." She looked at Darcy quickly and added, "Not the ones you write, of course."

"Of course."

"At least you can understand the words," Tyler said. "Rock is all noisy guitars and electronic sound effects."

"It is not," Jamaica denied hotly.

"Is, too."

"Is not."

One more "is, too" and Riley would scream, so he said cheerfully, "There are a lot of truly beautiful country songs."

"Name one," Jamaica challenged.

"Well, what about 'I Have Tears in My Ears from Lying on the Bed and Crying over You'?" Darcy suggested.

"Or how about the one where the guy says, 'If you want to keep the beer real cold, put it next to my ex-wife's heart'?" Tyler asked, giggling.

They all laughed and agreed on a compromise that would give both kinds of music equal airtime.

The children rode quietly for a while, taking in the unfamiliar scenery, but the sounds of too much sibling proximity soon filled the back seat again.

"Tyler, you geekazoid, you're breathing on me."

"Excu-u-se me. Maybe I'll just hold my breath and turn blue."

"I wish."

"Get your fat leg off my side of the seat," Tyler warned.

"Make me."

"I wouldn't waste the time."

"You drank my root beer, didn't you?" Jamaica accused.

"That was my root beer, megadunce. You had a cola."

"I did not."

"You did, too."

When Riley could stand it no longer, he told the kids to zip their lips and enjoy the ride. The next one who whined, nagged, griped or called his or her sibling a name would have to unload all the suitcases alone.

By the time they arrived at Roman Nose lodge, the beautiful golden day had given way to a drizzly rain. Riley hadn't thought reservations necessary and soon found the lodge was filled to capacity. Ignoring the looks of reproach from Darcy and the kids, he drove from one motel parking lot to another, only to find the No Vacancy sign lit up at every one.

"Is it just me," he asked. "Or does there seem to be an eerie amount of tourist trade for this time of year?"

"Maybe everyone had the same idea we did," Darcy offered.

At the very next motel, the manager explained the lack of accommodations. There was a Baptist Bible retreat being held at the lodge and all the local motels were taking up the overflow.

Riley got back in the car, wet, hungry and discouraged. He'd promised the kids a long nature hike in the afternoon, but the way it was raining now, that was out of the question. Darcy suggested they go home and come back another time when they remembered to make reservations, but Riley was determined not to give up.

"There's a Vacancy sign on that one," Tyler called out from his perch behind Darcy's ear.

"Good eye, Tyler." Riley made a U-turn and pulled into the bumpy parking lot of a rundown and nondescript establishment called the Blue Spruce Tourist Cabin Motel. Since there wasn't a single blue spruce in the vicinity, Riley assumed the name had either come out of the owner's optimism or his imagination. But dilapidated or not, the neon Vacancy sign winked and beckoned in the rain like a lighthouse in the fog.

Darcy refrained from expressing her opinion about why the cabins were vacant. The tiny buildings appeared to have been built long before the highway and were now nestled much too close to the road.

Jamaica wasn't so reticent. "This place hasn't been painted since Moby Dick was a minnow. Way to go, Tyler."

"It beats just drivin' around in this stupid rain all day. I wonder if it has cable."

Jamaica hooted. "We'll be lucky if it has electricity. It kinda reminds me of the Bates Motel. Remember *Psycho*, Tyler?" she asked in her best ghoul voice.

Even though he was a television fanatic, Tyler had a low threshold for horror movies. "It does not. It's a dump, but there's no monsters here. Are there, Riley?"

"Of course not. Now that's enough out of you two." But even he looked at the place with misgivings. "I'll ask to see the rooms before I decide. Agreed?"

"That sounds fair enough," Darcy answered before the children could start another argument. "We'll wait in the car."

"With the door locked," Tyler said uneasily.

"Watch out for guys with chain saws, Riley," Jamaica called out.

Although they weren't much to look at and didn't offer the luxuries of the lodge, the small two-bedroom cabins proved spotlessly clean and water tight. There was a tiny sitting room with a sofa bed, which Tyler immediately put dibs on.

Darcy figured that the coin-operated, black-and-white television set might have influenced his choice of beds. The anachronism, common to motels when she was a child, intrigued Tyler, a product of the electronic age and cable.

They brought in their luggage, and Riley suggested they drive back to Watonga and eat lunch at a steak house they'd noticed on their way through.

Everyone agreed but Tyler. He wanted to stay and watch the rest of an old western movie that he'd switched on upon arriving.

Darcy shrugged. "We can wait, I suppose."

Jamaica flopped down on a rickety chair that had probably been placed there sometime in the fifties. "That's selfish, Ty!"

"It's almost over. I want to see how it ends."

"That's easy. Henry Fonda gets killed in a massacre, and John Wayne rides off into the sunset."

"Jamaica! Now you've spoiled it," he yelled.

"So let's go eat. I didn't come all the way out here to the boonies where it's raining cats and dogs just to watch a darned old movie."

"Did you come all the way out here just to feed your face?" Tyler asked.

"Anything would be better than watching some dumb movie on a microscopic screen. It's giving me a headache," she complained.

"So don't look at it," Tyler groused. "Anyway, I'm paying for it with my own quarters."

Riley took a deep breath. "It isn't the end of the world. How much longer can it last?"

"Two cavalry charges, three Indian uprisings and a court-martial," Jamaica griped.

Tyler glanced at the television booklet. "An hour. Why don't ya'll just take Mary Sunshine and go on, so I can watch it in peace," Tyler said. "I can stay by myself. I've done it lots of times."

"No, you're not staying alone here." Riley was adamant. "Aren't you hungry?"

"You can bring me back something."

Darcy tried to solve the problem by suggesting that she would stay with Tyler while Jamaica and Riley brought back food for all of them. They could eat in the cabin, picnic style.

Riley didn't like it. "Either we all go or we all stay."

Sensing mutiny on Jamaica's part, Darcy tried again. "I'm really tired and I'd much rather take a long soak in the tub than drive to town."

Jamaica jumped to her feet. "Come on, Riley, let's blow this pop stand. I'm starving." He consented reluctantly and it wasn't long before he and Jamaica drove away.

Darcy told Tyler not to open the door for anyone and went off to run her bath water. She *was* tired, she thought with a secret smile. Riley had kept her awake late into the night showing her just how much he'd missed her. As she stripped off her damp clothes and sank into the warm water, she noted that it had finally stopped raining. Maybe there would still be time for that nature walk after they ate.

Relaxing in the warm water, she thought about Riley. He had told her over the phone that he wanted to talk, but now that they were together, he didn't seem to be in any hurry to do so. Of course, they never really got the chance. Maybe it was a good thing they kept busy and let the children monopolize their time.

Nothing was resolved, but in a way, avoiding the issue was avoiding conflict that might drive them apart for good.

Out in the sitting room, the Duke was still shooting up the territory, and Darcy leaned back against the back of the tub. Closing her eyes, she allowed the warm water to lull her into sleep. When she was startled awake, she realized that the television was quiet. Either the Duke had run out of bullets or Tyler had run out of quarters with which to plug the set.

"Tyler," she called.

No answer. Maybe he'd fallen asleep on the sofa.

She quickly toweled dry and slipped on the terrycloth robe she'd brought along. Stepping into the living room, she knew immediately something was wrong.

A quick inspection of the cabin told her that Tyler wasn't there. The front door was ajar.

Darcy flung on her clothes and slipped into her shoes. Grabbing a jacket, she ran to the office and asked the manager if he'd seen Tyler.

The old man behind the counter told her he had. "The lad was in here asking for change. When I told him I was plumb out, he wanted to know where he could get some. I told him he might try the service station about a half mile down the road."

Darcy thanked him and left. She jogged all the way to the service station, but it was closed. Dusk was closing in and she assumed Tyler would head for the cabin. She turned and raced back in the direction she'd come. She kept telling herself he was fine, that her growing worry was totally irrational, but she couldn't shake the maternal instinct that made her pulse pound.

Coming back from the restaurant with a bag full of charbroiled burgers on the seat between them, Riley and Jamaica spotted Darcy on the road just ahead. He could tell by her heaving chest and the frightened look on her face that she was not out for a pleasant evening stroll.

The car screeched to a halt, and Riley jumped out. Catching her in his arms, he demanded, "What happened?"

"It's Tyler." Darcy tearfully explained as best she could, and Riley tried to reassure her.

Jamaica climbed into the back seat so Darcy could have the front, and they drove back to the cabin.

"Don't worry, Darcy," the girl told her. "It's not like he's missing or anything."

"Of course he isn't missing," Riley said with some confidence. "I'll bet he's already back at the cabin wondering where you went."

But Tyler was not in their cabin, and a quick search revealed that he was nowhere on the grounds. None of the other guests or employees of the motel had seen him since he stopped by the office on his quarter quest.

"So what do we do now?" Darcy asked.

"I think we should call the authorities," Riley said solemnly.

"No!" Jamaica cried. "Don't do that."

"Honey, we have to. We can't find him by ourselves," Riley explained.

"But if you call the cops, it'll make it real. It'll mean Ty's really in trouble." Jamaica chewed on her thumbnail and looked beseechingly at the adults.

Riley didn't like to think about it, but he knew that in the case of a kidnapping, the first few hours were the most important. He looked at Darcy and Jamaica and knew he couldn't voice his concern. "It means we'll just find him that much faster."

He went to the office to make the necessary call and within twenty minutes, a uniformed officer from the sheriff's office arrived at the Blue Spruce. Deputy Rogers asked what seemed like a million questions. What did the boy look like? What was he wearing? Was he upset? Had there been any family problems prior to his disappearance? Did he have relatives in the area? Did he have any money and if so, how much?

Riley lost his patience. "It's starting to rain again, and Tyler's out there somewhere. I can't stand around here answering questions, I have to do something."

The deputy scribbled on his pad. "If he's a runaway—"

"It's all my fault," Jamaica cried. "I shouldn't have made such a fuss about the movie."

"What'd she do to the boy?" Deputy Rogers wanted to know.

"She didn't do anything," Riley yelled. "Dammit, Tyler is not a runaway! He's lost!"

Darcy wrapped her arms around the sobbing girl. "Don't cry, Jamaica," she soothed, wanting to cry herself. "If anyone's at fault here, it's me. I shouldn't have left him alone."

The deputy frowned. "I thought you said you were with the boy, Mrs. Sawyer."

"She was taking a bath. Tyler was watching a movie, but he ran out of quarters and went looking for change without letting my wife know." Riley knew he couldn't take much more of this.

"I see." The deputy closed his notebook and pocketed it. "He's been gone about an hour, then, is that right?"

"Yes," Riley agreed. "And since this is getting us absolutely nowhere, I'm going to retrace his steps and see if I can find him myself."

"Mr. Sawyer, I can't tell you not to go looking for your son, but I can tell you that it's easy to lose your sense of direction in the woods when you aren't used to the area. It'll be dark soon, so why don't you leave it to me and my men?"

"I just want to do something."

"Look, local reporters are going to pick this up on the police band. A little-boy-lost case like this is sure to generate a lot of attention that'll bring out civilian search teams. We'll put all the manpower on this we can, but I need you to stay here and be with your family. To talk to reporters. You can do that, can't you?''

As soon as Riley agreed, Deputy Rogers called for reinforcements. Riley took Darcy and Jamaica back to the cabin where Darcy turned on all the lights to try and dispel some of the gloom. Bright light didn't help. The spirits of the occupants were bleaker than any rainstorm.

Jamaica huddled on the sofa, tears streaming down her face. "What if they don't ever find him?"

Riley put his arm around her. "Don't worry, punkin, of course we'll find him. He'll be all right." He stood and reached for his jacket. "I can't just stay here, I'm going out to look for him."

"No, please," Jamaica begged. "Don't leave."

Fearing she was becoming hysterical, Darcy tried to comfort her, but Jamaica turned to Riley instead. "Everyone I've ever cared about leaves me. First Dad, then Mom. Now Tyler. Don't you leave me, too, Riley. I don't want to be alone."

Riley's eyes met Darcy's over the child's head, and he saw her stricken look. For the first time since their marriage, he knew exactly what she was thinking. That she still didn't count for much with Jamaica. That being with Darcy was the same as being alone. That the children knew that theirs was not a real family.

Later, when Tyler was safe and everyone was calm, he'd explain that Jamaica hadn't meant it the way it sounded. "I'm not leaving you, Jamaica," he told her. "I'm just going to look for Tyler."

Jamaica lifted her chin defiantly and swiped at her tears. "Okay," she said, getting stiffly to her feet. "I'll lie down in the bedroom for a while."

When the door closed behind her, Darcy looked up at Riley. "Why did this have to happen? I was making progress with her and now she blames me for Tyler being gone."

"She doesn't blame you, she's just upset is all."

"You heard what she said. I don't belong here."

"Don't ever say that, Darcy," he said fiercely. "We belong together. We always have and we always will."

"You're upset. Don't say things now that would best be taken up at a more appropriate time."

He ran his fingers through his hair, torn between wanting to find his son and needing to stay with his daughter. "I don't know what to do."

"You shouldn't leave her. Not like this. I'm sure the sheriff's department is doing everything possible."

"I know." He knocked on Jamaica's door.

"Go away," came the muffled reply.

"Come out here, punkin, we need you with us."

There was no answer.

"Please, Jamaica, we're a family. We have to stick together."

The door squeaked open, then Jamaica flung herself into Riley's arms. He reached out and drew Darcy into the embrace. No matter what happened, no matter how this night ended up, he was going to fight to keep his family together. Darcy might think she could leave him when six months were up, but she was wrong. He'd tried to hold her with love, but if that wouldn't work, he'd use whatever means he could.

But one thing was certain. The deal was off.

A pounding knock at the door broke the three of them apart. Riley and Darcy looked at each other for a desperate moment. If this was news, let it be good, their eyes seemed to say.

Riley opened the door and the yellow glow of the bug light outside revealed Deputy Rogers and a sheepish-looking Tyler. The boy was wet, but he didn't appear to be any the worse for wear. He had a can of cola in one hand and a candy bar in the other.

After a tearful reunion with his family, Tyler explained that when he found the service station closed, he'd set out for a diner farther down the road. He'd seen a raccoon on the side of the road and when it had darted into the woods, he'd followed hoping to get a closer look.

He'd quickly become disoriented. "But I didn't panic," he told them proudly. "In Cub Scouts we learned that if you get lost in the woods, you just hug a tree till somebody finds you."

Deputy Rogers laughed. "And that's what he was doing when one of my men discovered him. Hugging a tree. First thing he said was, 'What took you so long?'"

Jamaica, though obviously grateful to have her brother restored to her, couldn't resist teasing him. "We thought you were crow bait, you weenie. It's just like you to do something dumb and then wind up being the center of attention."

Tyler allowed Jamaica to ruffle his hair, but when she tried to kiss him, he ducked away. Evidently there was a limit to sibling tolerance even in extreme circumstances.

Chapter Eleven

Riley didn't have to put up the fight for Darcy that he had expected. When they got home, the events in Roman Nose Park seemed to bring the whole family closer together, and she no longer talked of not belonging. In fact, she didn't talk much at all. At least not about the issue of their marriage.

He switched the king-size bed in Tyler's room for the two twins in the master bedroom, explaining that the new arrangement would give the boy more room and be more comfortable when his friends started spending the night. Darcy accepted the change quietly.

Now that the quarter-horse racing season was over, he didn't have to travel, but he still had to put in a lot of time at the stables. The one-two victory at the Futurity had brought in new clients from around the country and the Sawyer men made plans to expand their operation. With Noelle so close to term, Brody didn't want to leave her any more than he had to, so it fell to Riley to meet with the architects and contractors they had called in.

The children were happy in school and during the parent-teacher conferences in mid-October, both received a good report card and praise from their teachers.

The retirement home Dub and Ruby were building at Lake Texoma was nearing completion and they were planning to move out of the big house at Phoenix Farms after Thanksgiving. Ross—who was taking over ownership of the breeding farm—and Glory would be moving in. Perfect timing since they had just announced that they were expecting their first child in the spring.

The clan was multiplying and there was peace in their world. Life was so good that it seemed to Riley that a generous and divine benefactor had taken control of their collective destinies. So why did he feel a sense of impending doom?

Even though he'd decided to let matters slide in the hope that things would take care of themselves, he knew he'd never feel safe until he had a firm commitment from Darcy. If she didn't offer one soon, he'd demand it.

It was nearly the end of October, the first frost of winter had finally put a bite into the air. Darcy was at the electronic piano, finishing the song that had been tugging at her subconscious all day. She'd never known such complete creative freedom before and it was a wonderful feeling to be able to sit down anytime she felt the urge to compose. Riley had made it all possible and she tried daily to let him know how much she appreciated him. She had taken an ostrich's approach to their problems, but since Tyler's rescue, her own insecurities seemed unimportant.

When Tyler and Jamaica called out from the living room that they were home, Darcy went to greet them.

"How was school?"

"The worst." Tyler flopped down on the couch.

"What's wrong?"

"Everybody's talking about trick-or-treating and I want to go, too, but there's not enough houses around here to make a good haul."

"That's so stupid." Jamaica rolled her eyes. "When are you going to grow up?"

"Make like a tree, Jamaica," Tyler told her, "and leave."

"I can see where trick-or-treating wouldn't be much fun out here," Darcy agreed. "Why don't we have a Halloween party and invite all your school friends."

The children loved the idea, and by the time Riley came in for supper they were full of enthusiasm. "Sounds like a lot of work to me," he said with a laugh.

"Not if we all pitch in," Darcy pointed out.

"Can it be a costume party?" asked Tyler.

"What else?" Darcy smiled. "It wouldn't be a Halloween party without costumes."

Riley shook his head. "I said I'd help, but I refuse to wear a dumb costume."

"But you have to. It's a rule," Jamaica said. "To get into the party you have to be in costume."

"You could come as a cowboy," suggested Tyler.

Jamaica frowned. "That's not a costume for Riley."

Darcy looked at him and raised a brow suggestively. "If you'll be a cowboy with a big gun, I'll be a dance-hall girl with a heart of gold."

That settled, the children went off to phone their friends with the news. Darcy trailed a finger across Riley's back. "You do have a big gun, don't you?"

Riley grabbed her around the waist and nibbled at her neck. "I'll wear my sidearms if you'll wear black stockings and garters—after the party."

Darcy put her arms around his neck and smiled up at him. "Sounds kinky to me."

"Yeah," he murmured against her lips.

The day of the party, Darcy was in the kitchen mixing punch when she received word that she had sold "Heart on the Line" to K. C. Maguire. Her agent was positive he could sell more if he had them and wanted to know when she could come to Nashville. The singer wanted to meet her and sign the deal in person.

Darcy agreed to call him the next day and set up an appointment. She hung up the phone just as Riley stepped into the kitchen.

"You look awfully happy for a lady up to her earlobes in orange punch and candy spiders."

She stirred the pumpkin-colored punch. "I sold 'Heart on the Line' and they want more."

Riley swung her around. "Congratulations!"

She kissed him hard. "Do you realize what this means?"

"Of course." He laughed. "You're going to be famous and I can retire to my palatial estate next door to Graceland."

She made a face. "It means, I don't have to worry about going back to the bank. I can take care of Mom's doctor bills and Cord's expenses myself."

Riley stiffened. "I thought that was my job."

"But don't you see? I won't be a financial drain on you anymore."

Hurt, Riley set her away from him. "I never thought of you as a financial drain, Darcy."

"I know, Riley, and you've already done much more than I can ever thank you for. But—"

"But what?"

"The six-month time limit on our marriage will be over soon and I don't want you to feel obligated."

Riley was ready to make his stand. To fight for the woman he loved. But her excitement and happiness about selling her song made him hesitant to take that moment away from her. Once more, he tabled the topic for later.

"I have to go to Nashville to meet K. C. Maguire. Can you believe it?"

"I believe it. I always knew you'd make it big. You just fooled me and did it a little quicker than I had expected."

The children ran in to tell Darcy that the caterers were setting up. Riley had insisted on having his favorite barbecue restaurant prepare and serve the food so that he and Brody wouldn't be deprived of their wives' company. What had started out as a party for the kids had snowballed into a major production when the adults refused to be left out of the fun.

Tyler and Jamaica, with the help of Dub and Ruby, had spent the day decorating the main barn with fake spider webs, honeycomb skeletons and fuzzy bats. They'd hung streamers and balloons, set up game booths and even a tape recorder and speakers for some appropriately spooky background music. The last time Darcy had checked on their progress they had certainly created a carnival atmosphere.

"I guess I'd better get into my costume," Riley remarked. He was as determined not to let his bad mood spoil the party for the kids as he was not to spoil Darcy's excitement over her sale.

"The party doesn't start for another two hours. It won't take you that long to get dressed." Darcy knew Riley had something on his mind, but this was neither the time nor the place to get to the bottom of it.

Tonight was supposed to be festive, and he was damned if he wouldn't have a good time. "It will if I'm going to help you get into those stockings," he said, his eyes twinkling.

The party was a huge success if noise and laughter were any measurement. The guests arrived early and stayed late. They ate barbecued foods, bobbed for apples, had their fortunes told, played games and generally had a great time.

The mother of one of Jamaica's friends was talking to Darcy and Riley, who were resplendent in their Dodge City outfits. "You know," the woman said, "you've probably started something. This was so much fun, you'll have to make it an annual event."

Darcy gave her a bright smile and agreed. But inside she was struggling with the knowledge that she probably wouldn't be here next year.

As another young guest left, Darcy overheard her telling Jamaica and Tyler that it was the best party she'd ever been to. "And your mom and dad are so nice," she gushed. "I just loved their costumes. Well, I'll see you at school tomorrow and maybe we could go to the movies together on Saturday."

To Darcy's unending surprise, Tyler and Jamaica merely thanked their friend without bothering to correct the child's mistaken assumption. "I'll ask my parents about the movie," Jamaica responded to the invitation.

Darcy fought tears. Mom and Dad. Parents. How could she keep living this charade?

Long after all the guests had left and the children were in bed, Darcy found Riley in the kitchen drinking a glass of milk. "I think everyone had a good time tonight, don't you?" she asked as she sat down at the table with him.

He nodded. He was afraid to talk for fear all the roiling emotions inside him would erupt.

"You're awfully quiet. Is something wrong?" she asked.

"I was just wondering when you were planning to leave?"

She swallowed hard. "Leave?"

"For Nashville."

She let out the breath she'd been holding. "I told my agent I'd let him know. I want to be here when Noelle has the baby so I can take care of the twins, do the bookkeeping and help her when she gets home again. Since she's due any day, it should be soon."

He stared into his glass of milk. "How long do you plan to be away?"

"No more than three or four days. Is there a problem?"

"Of course not, take all the time you need." Riley smiled as he stood and held out his hand. "With all the plans you have, you need to get some rest." He'd have as much of her as he could. For as long as he could.

Darcy grinned as she placed her hand in his. "Rest? Is that what we're going to do?"

In an obvious effort to accommodate everyone, Noelle went into labor that very night. When Brody called to say they were leaving for the hospital, Riley got up and went to fetch Dusty and Danny. The sleepy twins weren't sure what was going on, but they sensed something important was about to happen and that they were being excluded.

Darcy settled them in Tyler's room and had just returned to bed when Brody called with the happy news that they had barely made it to delivery before his daughter, Caitlyn, was born.

"Should we wake up the boys and tell them they have a new sister?" Darcy asked Riley.

"They're exhausted, let them sleep. Knowing them, they'd insist on seeing her tonight." Unlike his, Brody's family had the rest of their lives to be together.

Noelle recovered quickly from the birth and was out of the hospital in two days. In a couple of weeks, she was back in the ranch office with little Caitlyn sleeping in a cradle at her side. Darcy was enchanted by the baby and kept putting off her trip to Nashville, but finally, during the second week of November, her agent insisted she firm up her plans and she agreed to go.

She was looking on the top closet shelf for her travel iron when she found the bottle of whiskey. She held it in her hands and was still staring at it in disbelief when Riley came into the room to check on her packing.

"What's this?" she demanded in a tight voice.

He looked it over carefully as if trying to figure out a complicated puzzle. "Is that a trick question?"

"Riley! What is this?"

"A bottle of seven-year-old Kentucky bourbon, according to the label." He was trying to remain calm, but her suspicious attitude and harsh questions made him want to yell back that it was none of her business.

"What's it doing in our closet?" Darcy had stopped worrying about Riley ever drinking again and now here was evidence that might mean she'd been wrong all along.

"I put it there."

"Why? Why does a reformed alcoholic and a teetotaler need a bottle of bourbon?"

"Darcy, will you shut up a minute and listen to me?" Riley raked his fingers through his hair, half tempted to let her think the worst of him since she was obviously bent on doing just that. "Is the seal on that bottle broken?"

Quick examination revealed that it was not and she felt immense relief until she realized that if there could be one untouched bottle in the house, there could be empty ones, as well. She said as much.

"Not that I have to explain my actions to you, Miss Independence," he said crossly, "But I keep that bottle around as a test of my strength."

"I don't understand." She sat down on the bed.

"There's an old saying about virtue being the lack of temptation. I haven't said anything, but you know how protective everyone is of me, especially Brody. At the wedding party, he practically hovered over me to make sure I didn't dip into the wrong punch bowl."

"He's just concerned."

"I know that. But the point is, as long as I keep that unopened bottle around, I know he doesn't have to be. Do you understand?"

"I suppose so. I'm sorry if I jumped to conclusions."

"Forget it." He turned to leave the room.

"Riley? You do understand why I'm going to Nashville, don't you?"

"Yeah. You need to make the contacts that are important to your career. You need to know that when you walk out of here in February, you'll have some financial security. That was our agreement, wasn't it? I got a wife for six months, and you got what you needed."

"That's not it," she cried in dismay.

"It's what you've always wanted. Marrying me was just a temporary detour on your road of life. God, now *I* sound like a country song. Look, you just have three more months to stick out, then you can go like we agreed. But I mean to hold you to it, Darcy. You don't have to share my bed, but by God, you'll hold up your end of the bargain."

Hurt beyond words, Darcy could only stare at him. This moment was the one she had feared most. The moment she would know for sure that she was no more to him than a convenience.

"All right, Riley, if that's the way you want it."

"That's the way I want it." When he left the room, he heard Jamaica's door close quietly, but was too preoccupied to think much of it.

Darcy left Oklahoma City on a cold, winter-bitter day.

The children were strangely subdued in her absence, and even Beany moped around the house looking for her.

"Beany's not eating," Tyler told Riley. "Do you think he's missing Darcy, too?"

"Probably. He'll be fine when she gets home," Riley told him.

"But when is Darcy coming back and how long does it take a dog to starve?"

"I don't know," Riley admitted. "But we can call Aunt Glory and ask her."

"She's a horse doctor," Tyler said.

"Dummy, she had to study dogs, too." Jamaica had become sullen of late. "Darcy *is* coming back, isn't she?"

"Of course she is," Riley insisted. He knew he should come clean with the kids, but he didn't know how. "I told you she'd be home for Thanksgiving." Jamaica's question unnerved him. "So why do you ask?"

Jamaica shrugged and turned her attention back to the television. "Just checking."

* * *

Darcy hadn't planned to stay in Nashville as long as she did, but one meeting led to another and before long, K. C. Maguire wanted enough songs to fill an album.

The trouble was, the singer insisted on discussing her own ideas at long, smoky brainstorming sessions so that when Darcy went home, she could complete the work quickly. To that end, she invited Darcy to stay with her and her husband while she was in town.

Darcy could hardly refuse. A newcomer like herself didn't dare turn down the hospitality of a star like K. C. Maguire.

After a few days, Darcy decided that she might as well kill two birds with one stone. While she was trying to come up with song ideas that pleased K.C., she could just get used to being lonely.

Chapter Twelve

On Thanksgiving Day, Noelle's kitchen was filled with the women of the family and their combined contributions to the holiday meal. The men were holed up in the den cheering their favorite football teams to victory, but they occasionally sent a runner for snacks and beer.

It had been a solemn Riley who had picked up Darcy at the airport the night before. He'd expressed a passing interest in her trip, willing to listen but not to talk. It was as if he had already dismissed her from his life.

Considering how difficult the next few weeks would be, she decided it was just as well. He seemed filled with some of his old grimness, but she was too busy trying to put on a happy and unaffected appearance to confront him about his moods.

The morning had passed quickly, dedicated as it was to visiting and food preparation. But soon everyone would crowd around the dining room table to thank the good fortune that allowed them all to be together. Then they would attempt to consume a mountain of food that couldn't possibly be eaten in a week, much less in one meal.

Now, as Darcy glanced around at all the cooks in the kitchen, she offered to look in on the baby. Just before she could slip into the nursery, she met Riley in the hall.

"Are you sneaking away for some peace and quiet?" he asked. "This family can get pretty wild when we're all together. But I guess you won't have to worry about that much longer."

She let the snide comment go unremarked. "I told Noelle I'd check on the baby."

"Mind if I come along? I'd like another look at my new niece."

Darcy had wanted to be alone, but she could hardly deny Riley's request.

They stopped outside the nursery door when they heard low voices inside. Riley was about to knock when he realized the voices belonged to Jamaica and Tyler.

"If Riley and Darcy have a baby, what would it be to us?" they heard Tyler whisper.

"First of all, it wouldn't be anything to us, because technically we aren't any relation to them."

His sister's authoritative tone made Tyler come back defensively. "They're our parents."

"Not legally. It's not written down anywhere."

"Riley said there would be a hearing or something and then he'd be our guardian."

"A guardian isn't the same as a parent," Jamaica was quick to point out.

"So their baby wouldn't be our brother or sister?" Tyler was persistent.

"They won't be having a baby," Jamaica was just as quick to assure him.

"They might, Jamaica. You don't know everything."

"Take my word for it. There's not going to be any baby."

"You think you know everything," he said accusingly. "When we first came here, you said Darcy wouldn't like us and she'd make Riley send us off to a foster home. And when she didn't, you said we wouldn't be staying because Riley had a drinking problem, but he doesn't."

"Well," Jamaica said defensively, "he used to."

"Riley has never lied to us like Mom did, and you know it. He told us that he stopped drinking last year and he wants us all to be a family."

"Well, he may not drink anymore but he lied about wanting to be a family," his sister said bitterly. "He and Darcy won't even be married after February. I heard them talking about it before she left for Nashville."

"I don't believe you," Tyler cried vehemently. A note of fear had crept into his voice.

"I didn't want to believe it, either, but it's true."

"We were pretty bad when we first came," Tyler admitted unhappily. "Do you think if maybe we're real nice and help a lot, she'd stay?"

"You're such a hopeless baby, Tyler." Jamaica's sigh was audible to the eavesdroppers outside. "They didn't even want to get married. Riley needed to have a wife, and Darcy needed money or something. I don't know exactly, but they made a deal and it will be over in February."

"What about us?"

"Maybe we'll stay with Riley. Then again, who knows?"

"But what about Darcy? I want her to stay, too."

"So do I, but I don't think we should plan on it."

Darcy's heart clutched up as the children revealed their fears. She was responsible for their insecurity. She never thought they'd care enough to be hurt by her leaving. She glared at Riley for his part in the mess they'd created. "I guess it's true that eavesdroppers never hear good of themselves. It's time for you to talk honestly with those kids."

"What am I supposed to tell them?" Riley felt things spinning out of control. This was not supposed to happen. This day was never supposed to come.

"I don't know. Try the truth," she advised as he opened the door.

After Riley and the children left the nursery to talk privately, Darcy wiped away her tears. Looking down at tiny Caitlyn, sleeping peacefully with a small, perfect fist curled against her cheek, she realized how fragile children were.

Jamaica and Tyler had needed stability, and she and Riley had made a grave mistake by allowing them to believe that she could fill a space in their lives. That it was done out of love might not be enough to justify the bungled results.

It had been selfish of her to marry Riley in the first place. She should have been strong enough to let him go. She never should have let her foolish heart run her life off course. Why hadn't she realized all the impossibilities of the situation? Maybe it wasn't love that made a person blind, after all. Maybe it was hope.

Caitlyn awoke, and Darcy gently lifted the pink-wrapped bundle into her arms. She breathed in the sweet baby fragrance, touched the unbelievably soft skin. She'd had such hopes, and one of them was that someday she and Riley might give Jamaica and Tyler a little brother or sister, a child who would make their family circle complete. Hope, there it was again. It did have a tendency to get in the way of reality.

Riley slipped silently into the nursery. As unsure as he'd been, he felt he'd handled the situation well. First, he'd assured the children that he loved them and wanted to take whatever legal steps were necessary to make sure no one could ever take them away. He would adopt them and, as Sawyers, they would have a life-long undisputed place in the family.

They were happy and relieved about that news, but then he tried to explain his arrangement with Darcy. Jamaica acted as if it were all she could expect from adults, but Tyler would not accept that Darcy might leave.

"Does she *want* to go away?" he had demanded. "Did you actually ask her and did she actually say she didn't want to stay? Did she?"

In his efforts to explain to his son, Riley had realized that Darcy had never said in so many words that she *wanted* to abide by the temporary marriage. "Not exactly," he'd told Tyler.

The little boy had grinned triumphantly. "See! I told you. You never asked her so you can't know."

Jamaica had perked up, as well, "Maybe the twerp's right. Maybe if you ask her to stay, she will."

That solution sounded much too simple to solve such a complicated problem, but Riley was desperate enough to try anything.

When he cleared his throat to announce his presence, Darcy whirled around with Caitlyn in her arms.

"Did you talk to them?" she asked.

"Yes, I told them the truth."

"How did they take it?"

"They wouldn't accept it." He related the conversation.

"So you came here on their behalf to ask me to stay, is that it?" She laid the baby back into the crib and turned to face Riley.

"No. I came here on my own behalf to ask you to stay. For the time being, let's just leave the kids out of it. This isn't about them."

"I thought it was *all* about them. Aren't they the reason you asked me to marry you in the first place?"

"They were the excuse I used, but they were not the reason. Dammit, Darcy, I don't know what to say."

For such a strong man, he could really tie himself up in knots. "You sure didn't have any trouble coming up with bright ideas that night in the Dust Bowl." Darcy recalled that conversation and her frustration grew. "How were you planning to handle things when it came time for us to part company?"

"I was hoping that wouldn't come up," he admitted honestly. "I thought I was doing everything right. I quit drinking, I did my best to take care of you, I did everything possible to show you I love you. I—"

"Never told me," came her whispered interruption.

"What?"

"You never told me you loved me."

"I did so."

"You did not."

"I must have."

"You told me you wanted me. You told me you needed me. You even told me you were grateful that I married you. But not once did you ever say, 'Darcy, I love you.'" She watched the baby, not Riley.

Shocked awareness rendered him momentarily speechless. Had he been so careful not to rush her that he'd failed to let her know how much he cared? "I held back because I wanted to prove myself before I asked for your love."

She gripped the side of the crib to steady herself.

"Riley, you idiot! You didn't have to prove anything and you didn't have to ask. I've always loved you. I never stopped. But I thought you just needed me to get the children. That all you really wanted was a housekeeper, a baby-sitter."

"Now who's the idiot?" He pulled her into his arms and held her tightly, eager to make up for his stupidity. "I thought I was doing the right thing."

"I thought you were acting," she admitted.

He laughed at that. "Darlin', if I was that good an actor I wouldn't have to train horses." He held her face in his hands. "Darcy, I love you. I want to live with you and have children with you. I want to grow old and gray with you. Corny as it sounds, I want us to leave our dentures on the same shelf when we go to bed at night."

He took a long look at her and continued.

"Darcy, I love you." Now that he'd said it, he couldn't stop. "If you'll stay with me, I'll spend the rest of my life saying it, showing it and proving it. Hell, I'll paint it on the side of the barn for the whole world to see."

Darcy was laughing and crying as she offered him her love and her trust. "I want all those things, too. But I was kinda hoping we could keep our real teeth."

Once everyone was seated around the table, Noelle asked Dub to carve the turkey and uphold the family tradition that required each member to tell the others what he or she was most thankful for.

Dub stood and cleared his throat. "I ain't a man who usually makes long speeches, but dang it, I looked around this here table and figured it might just take me a while to say what all I'm thankful for. I know I start out with this every year, but the first thing I'm glad of is Ruby. The old girl and I have weathered good times and bad, but even the bad ones were halfway fun because we had each other. That's something I hope every one of you young people will remember."

He shifted his weight and continued talking and carving. "We thought the good Lord was only gonna see fit to bless us with one child, our Glory. But then He heard our prayers and He sent us two boys to raise, Brody and Riley. We always thought that was His way of making up for keepin' us waiting so long. Then, when I was praying some poor fool would come along and take my wayward gal off my hands, He sent me Ross. Another son."

When everyone stopped laughing, he went on. "Another thing I'm grateful for is that all my children had the good sense to marry well." He grinned at Noelle, Ross and Darcy. "They couldn't have picked better if they'd ordered out of a catalog." He started passing the plates of turkey around the table.

"Now we got us a whole new generation coming up." His fond gaze took in Danny, Dusty, Jamaica, Tyler and little Caitlyn, and lingered on Glory who would give him his next grandchild. "I got me a feeling that good things are in store for this family."

He sat down self-consciously. Ruby sniffed loudly before she spoke up. "That all goes double for me."

In turn, each person at the table had his or her say.

Holding her husband's hand, Glory smiled and said, "I'm thankful that Ross finally let me catch him."

Ross agreed with her and said he was grateful to be part of such a wonderful family. "I'm thankful for everything Dub and Ruby have given me. Especially their daughter."

When it was Brody's turn, he elected to be brief. Cradling his baby daughter in his big arms, he said, "I'm thankful this little one arrived safely." Recalling how he and Noelle had met, he grinned and added, "I'm also thankful Noelle dialed the wrong number that day."

Noelle touched his hand and smiled lovingly. "I'm just thankful Brody didn't mind being cussed out so early in the morning and decided to look me up."

Darcy's mother, Ida, and her brother, Cord, both acknowledged their appreciation of Riley's help and of being included in the family traditions.

Danny was thankful for his new sister, and Dusty was thankful that the talking was almost over—he was hungry.

Tyler said he was thankful to be back at Cimarron. Jamaica looked at Riley and Darcy holding hands so happily and beamed. "I'm thankful for my new parents."

Then it was Riley's turn. He had so much to be thankful for that he hardly knew where to begin. "I guess everyone knows I'm thankful just to be here. And for the 413 days of sobriety that made it possible. There was a time when my future didn't look too bright. Then I met Darcy and she gave me a reason to make more of my life than I ever thought it could be." He smiled at her, and the love shone in his eyes.

"I've always considered Jamaica and Tyler the children of my heart and I'm thankful that very soon now they will also be mine in the eyes of the law." He squeezed his wife's hand and sat down.

With everyone gazing expectantly at her, Darcy was at a loss to express herself. She had so many things, so many people, to be thankful for. So much happiness to look forward to. So many bright tomorrows. When she stood to speak, she summed it all up in one sentence.

"I am thankful for forever."

* * * * *

Take 4 bestselling love stories FREE

Plus get a FREE surprise gift!

From *New York Times* Bestselling author
Penny Jordan, a compelling novel of ruthless passion
that will mesmerize readers everywhere!

Penny Jordan

Silver

Real power, true power came from
Rothwell. And Charles vowed to have it,
the earldom and all that went with it.

Silver vowed to destroy Charles, just as surely and
uncaringly as he had destroyed her father; just as he had
intended to destroy her. She needed him to want her . . .
to desire her . . . until he'd do anything to have her.

But first she needed a tutor: a man who wanted no one.
He would help her bait the trap.

**Played out on a glittering international stage,
Silver's story leads her from the luxurious comfort of
British aristocracy into the depths of adventure,
passion and danger.**

AVAILABLE NOW!

 **HARLEQUIN**

SIL-1A

Win 1 of 10 Romantic Vacations and Earn Valuable Travel Coupons Worth up to $1,000!

Inside every Harlequin or Silhouette book during September, October and November, you will find a PASSPORT TO ROMANCE that could take you around the world.

By sending us the official entry form available at your favorite retail store, you will automatically be entered in the PASSPORT TO ROMANCE sweepstakes, which could win you a star-studded London Show Tour, a Carribean Cruise, a fabulous tour of France, a sun-drenched visit to Hawaii, a Mediterranean Cruise or a wander through Britain's historical castles. The more entry forms you send in, the better your chances of winning!

In addition to your chances of winning a fabulous vacation for two, valuable travel discounts on hotels, cruises, car rentals and restaurants can be yours by submitting an offer certificate (available at retail stores) properly completed with proofs-of-purchase from any specially marked PASSPORT TO ROMANCE Harlequin® or Silhouette® book. The more proofs-of-purchase you collect, the higher the value of travel coupons received!

For details on your PASSPORT TO ROMANCE, look for information at your favorite retail store or send a self-addressed stamped envelope to:

PASSPORT TO ROMANCE
P.O. Box 621
Fort Erie, Ontario L2A 5X3

ONE PROOF-OF-PURCHASE

3-CSR-2

To collect your free coupon booklet you must include the necessary number of proofs-of-purchase with a properly completed offer certificate available in retail stores or from the above address.

© 1990 Harlequin Enterprises Limited